All Eyes On The Crown 3:

Rise of A New Connect

Tina J

Copyright 2017

This novel is a work of fiction. Any resemblances to actual events, real people, living or dead, organizations, establishments or locales are products of the author's imagination. Other names, characters, places, and incidents are used fictionally.

More Books by Tina J

A Thin Line Between Me & My Thug 1-2
I Got Luv for My Shawty 1-2
Kharis and Caleb: A Different kind of Love 1-2
Loving You is a Battle 1-3
Violet and the Connect 1-3
You Complete Me
Love Will Lead You Back
This Thing Called Love
Are We in This Together 1-3
Shawty Down to Ride For a Boss 1-3
When a Boss Falls in Love 1-3
Let Me Be The One 1-2
We Got That Forever Love
Ain't No Savage Like The One I got 1-2
A Queen & Hustla 1-2 (collab)
Thirsty for a Bad Boy 1-2
Hasaan and Serena: An Unforgettable Love 1-2
We Both End Up With Scars
Are We in this Together 1-3
Caught up Luvin a beast 1-3
A Street King & his Shawty 1-2
I Fell for the Wrong Bad Boy 1-2 (collab)
Addicted to Loving a Boss 1-3
I need that Gangsta Love 1-2 (collab)
Still Luvin' a Beast 1-2
I Wanna Love You 1-2
When She's Bad, I'm Badder 1-3

Table of Contents:

Previously…

MJ

"Is everything in place?" I asked Alex who had just come back from the states. He was in hot water with Gabby over the bullshit PJ said. Yes, he was over here with Julia but like my brother said, it had nothing to with him sleeping with her.

We found out she had been in contact with some people and was trying to have Gabby killed. She was obsessed with my brother and refused to allow him to be happy. Unfortunately for her, she forgot who we were. The same person she asked to commit the murder, is the same guy who worked for us.

See everyone assumed we had lieutenants and didn't know who was on our team. That's never the case. Anyone hired to join anything with the name Rodriquez on it, had to be checked out thoroughly. I'm talking about parents, grandparents, ancestors, friends, foes and anyone else affiliated with them.

A few times we went to the their houses if they had dogs to see how certain individuals handled them. Are they friendly with their pets or abusive? Shit, like that can tell a lot about a person. It may sound crazy but the way people take care of animals can show how they are in situations too.

"Yea. You ready." I stood up and grabbed my things to leave.

"What you going to do now that you found out it's true? You think Morgan will be ok?" I ran my hand over my head.

"I don't know but one thing I know for sure, is her ass ain't leaving me." He nodded his head and sat back staring out the window. I removed my phone out my pocket and looked at the text.

Wife: *I can't wait to see you. I miss you.* Morgan was still in the states visiting her family, who was ecstatic when they found out I proposed.

Me: *I miss you too.* I opened up the next message and was blown away. Morgan had on a one-piece lingerie set with some fuck me heels on. Her leg was on a chair and her fingers were in her pussy. I got a video right after and there was no way in hell, I could open it with my brother sitting next to me.

Me: *Bring that ass home TONIGHT*! I put the phone in my pocket when the truck came to a stop.

"It's time." Alex said and both of us stepped out.

I opened the door, let my feet hit the ground and stretched my arms up. This is one of the moments I've been waiting for. It took me some time to find what's behind the door but now that the truth is out, it was worth the search.

I walked in and down the hallway with a smile on my face. I couldn't believe it's been six months and I was coming face to face with the person I never met. One of the guards opened the door and there she was in a pack and play looking like my daughter, her sister Arcelia. She turned around and put her little hands up for me to hold her. It was funny because this is my first time meeting her. I guess she knows who her father is. I sat her on my lap and thought about how I found them.

"MJ, what are you doing here? How... did you..." Carlotta *asked when she stepped out the shower and noticed me on the bed.*

"Is that anyway to greet the man you claimed to love? Or the man you violated and stole sperm from?"

"MJ, you enjoyed it." She said as if she tried to believe it herself. I ran over to the wall she refused to move from.

"Bitch, you drugged me and..." she cut me off.

"I'm sorry. I love you and.-"

"Love would've never allowed you to almost kill me, just to have my kid. Matter of fact, where is the baby?"

9

"MJ please."

"You know how I feel about people begging once they get caught." As soon as I said that, we heard a baby cry.

"Alex, get the baby and take her to abuela's. The doctor will be there shortly to take a DNA." He nodded and did what I asked. I didn't want to look at her and become attached. What if she weren't mine? Even though she resembled Le Le in the photos, it could still be a coincidence. I heard the front door close and got down to business with Carlotta.

"MJ, please don't take my baby. I swear, I won't bother you or.-" I put my finger to her lips and let it roam down to her neck, the top of her chest and soon after unwrapped the towel for what's to come next. Carlotta was indeed a bad bitch but she fucked up violating me.

"If that's my baby, Morgan will be her mother. There will be no memories of you whatsoever. It will be as if Morgan birthed her."

"How when they are close in age?" They were only a week apart from what she said in all the messages she would send.

"That's right. Well, I'll have it put on paper that they're fraternal twins. Thanks for reminding me. I would hate to have Camila grow up, unsure about things."

"Who is Camila?"

"Oh that's my daughter's name if she's mine."

"But that's not what I named her."

"Ugh, do you really think I care? Plus, since they're going to be considered twins, their name should be similar. Now, lets get to what's about to happen."

"MJ please." She was hysterical crying as she begged for her life when the two guys stepped in.

"Carlotta, I was good to you. I never treated you like shit, you held it down in the bedroom and I gave you what you wanted as far as money, gifts an other shit."

"I didn't want any of it. I only wanted you." I had to laugh. She said that but didn't return a damn thing or showed me any different.

"Carlotta, you know who I am. What, you thought because of the child it would make me feel sorry?" I nodded my head and the two guys made their way to her.

"What the fuck are they doing? Get off me."

"Oh these are some people on my team that are going to do the same thing to you, that you did to me." I stood there laughing and watching her try to fight them off.

"You're going to let them rape me?"

"This isn't rape Carlotta." I made my way over to her as one guy started to take his shirt off.

"It's what you want. Don't worry, you'll enjoy it." Her mouth dropped open. I walked out the room and sat in the living room waiting for them to finish. Call me what you want but the Bible says, do unto others as you want done to you. Now who am I not to give Carlotta exactly what she gave me? I mean granted, it's a little different but I wouldn't be MJ if I took it easy.

After a while both dudes came out slapping hands with one another without a care in the world. They informed me of how good of a time they both had.

Phew! Phew!

I shot both of them in the head, stepped over their bodies and went in the room. You ask why I did that when they were only doing what I asked. Well, if a man will rape a woman for his boss, he'll rape anyone. I can't have those two running around my streets thinking it's ok.

I opened the bedroom door and Carlotta was laid out. She was beaten so bad her face was unrecognizable. Her body

13

had bruises on it and blood was leaking from down below. I

stared at her, pointed my gun at her forehead and emptied my

entire clip in her body. I felt no remorse for taking away my

daughters mother and no one was going to make me.

Now I'm sitting here in my abuela's house holding my daughter for the first time. I felt a tear fall down my face as I stared. Carlotta made me miss out on a lot of time with her, all because she was being petty.

Camila clapped her hands and sucked on her binky as she stared at me. I removed it and I swear her and Le Le were definitely twins. I picked up my phone and called Morgan. I planned on waiting for her to get here to mention it but I wanted to see where her head was.

"Hey baby." She answered in a sexy voice.

"Hey. You coming home tonight?"

"Yup. Le Le and I are getting ready now. She misses her daddy and I miss him too." I laughed in the phone. Morgan was definitely a nympho.

"Babe, I need you to sit down for a minute."

"Is everything ok?" She instantly went into panic mode.

"Yea. I'm going to face time you but I need you to be ok with what you see."

"Miguel, if you're hurt, I don't want to see it. I'm leaving now and.-"

"Relax baby. I'm fine. Just answer when I call." I went to dial her number back and heard some commotion at my abuela's door. I stood up and walked down the hall to see what was going on.

"WHAT THE FUCK ARE YOU DOING HERE?" My daughter jumped from the bass in my voice. At this moment I was pissed for telling my security not to follow me here. I didn't want anyone around me when I met my daughter for the first time. I heard my phone with the face time ring tone. I must've been taking too long to call Morgan back.

"What I should've done a long time ago." I felt a sharp pain.

"Did you just shoot me with my daughter in my arms?" I looked and my abuela was on the ground.

"Look at it this way. You don't care who you kill so when I take her life, we can call it even." Another shot was fired and all I saw was red.

Alex

"What the fuck was that?" I said to my pops on the phone. He and I were discussing the accident with Gabby and who could be behind it.

Yea, she still isn't fucking with me but I make sure someone is watching her at all times. Especially now more than ever, since she has my kids in her stomach. I couldn't believe she was having twins. It didn't run in our family and hers either as far as I know, but I'm not complaining.

"What's going on?" My father was always on point when it came to family. When he heard me say that, I could hear him telling my mom they had to get over here.

"It sounded like a gunshot."

"A gunshot. Check on your brother and my mother. We'll be there in a few minutes." He hung the phone up in my ear.

I walked in the house from being on the back porch and saw Logan pointing a gun at my brother, who had my niece in his arms. Her back was turned so she had no idea I was coming. My grandmother was on the floor and Camila was crying.

"How could you have kids with someone else and made me terminate ours?" Once she said that, I knew this was over him not wanting her.

"Logan, I'm not about to debate shit with you. Its been over for a long time. Now you have a gun pointing at me and my daughter." I moved in closer but MJ gave me a look not to.

"MJ, I loved you. How could you do this to me." MJ was on the bottom step with my niece still in his hands. Logan had tears flowing down her face and her hair was all over her head. This is not the Logan I'm used to seeing.

"Logan, put the gun away or else." My brother told her but she didn't flinch.

"Or else what? Fuck you! At least we'll be even."

Time was of the essence when I heard her say she's about to take another life. At this point, she wasn't hearing anything my brother had to say. I pulled my gun out, pointed it and shot her. I didn't want to kill her because my brother did care for her at one time. If he wanted her dead it was on him.

Once she hit the ground, he handed me my niece and rushed over to Logan. I'm thinking he's about to call someone to help, but he started beating the shit out of her. He stood up and stomped her in the face over and over.

I grabbed his arm to try and stop him but he was in a zone. Not only that, I noticed blood on my hand. I ran and put my niece in the playpen, crying an all but I had to check on him and my grandmother.

"Abuela are you ok?" I was helping her off the ground and both of us jumped when we heard a gunshot go off. MJ stood over Logan with a sad look in his eyes but you could tell he had no remorse. He looked at us, then Camila and passed out.

"Oh my God Miguel. Get my baby some help." My mom screamed when she came running in. She put his head on her lap and kept telling him to stay with her.

"What the fuck happened?" My father was pissed and ran to my brother.

"I came in and Logan had a gun pointed at him."

"The stupid bitch hit me over the head. I'm glad he killed her psycho ass." My abuela was pissed and talking shit at the same time. She's never been one to bite her tongue.

"Miguel where are they? My son is bleeding to death." My mom was hysterical and not even five seconds later, in walked two big dudes who lifted MJ up and placed him on the kitchen table. The doctor came in and went to work. He told my dad he was only going to stabilize him here because he needed to get over to the spot where all his medical materials were.

I called Morgan on the phone and told her to get to Puerto Rico as soon as possible. Of course she was hysterical and ready to kill Logan, who I hadn't told her was already dead. My next call was to her security she knew nothing about and told them to make sure nothing happens to her. If it did, that's their ass. I'm positive they remember what happened to the last two.

I followed my parents over to the spot thinking about Gabby and how I wasn't there enjoying her pregnancy. Yes, I can go to the states if I want but MJ would be mad as hell if I left without him. I promised I wouldn't go if he weren't around and I didn't want to go and something happen. When he woke up and was feeling better I definitely planned on taking a trip.

I saw my parents go in the building at the spot and decided to make a U-turn and go to finish what I started. I parked and went inside to see my victim had used the bathroom in the chair. The room smelled horrible but its what happens when you're tied up.

"How are you Julia?" She woke up at the sound of my voice.

"It seems like you had an accident." I laughed and she rolled her eyes.

I removed the tape off her mouth and listened to her scream. The tape not only hurt to come off but it also tore the skin. Yea, I had this glue that could remove anything and well, it definitely works. Blood was leaking and I could see her teeth. It looked pretty crazy but I didn't expect anything different.

"Julia, you should've left my girl alone when you had the chance; instead I'm about to take your life for it." She shook her head no and the blood was flying everywhere.

"I should feel bad but because you've started so many unnecessary problems, I don't." She started crying.

"Bitch, don't cry now. Your ass wasn't doing that when you put a hit on his girl." Ricky said coming out the back with the machete I asked him to get. As he was going in on her, I began putting on something to cover my clothes, and shoes.

I knew my cousin was here because he had to do something for my aunt. I had him get the room ready for me but before I took her in there, I wanted her to feel pain. You don't fuck with me and get an easy death. Nah, in my mind, a person should suffer before taking their last breath to feel what's it like.

"This is for you opening your mouth to set up a hit on my girl." I took her tongue out and chopped it off.

I didn't waste anytime and cut off both of her hands. She almost passed out. I dragged her chair in the room and placed her in the center. This was going to be the best part. I backed away and shut the light on. Her body started to melt right before my eyes. I fucking loved it and recorded it on my phone. I would eventually show Gabby but until then, I'd keep it.

"Damnnnnnnnn, that shit looks crazy." Ricky said and called out for Pablo. He came walking over and smiled when he saw what Julia had become.

Pablo is a freak of nature and enjoyed seeing people this way. He got a kick out of it and would ask us to come watch if we had nothing to do. His ass would do nasty shit to them though and sometimes it made me sick.

"I'm out yo." I took my stuff off and dumped it in the inferno.

"How's Gabby?" I shrugged my shoulders.

"Alex, I don't know who's worse out of you and MJ."

"Oh that reminds me." I started telling him what went down at abuela's house and he ended up driving over to the spot with me to check on him.

The entire ride he got on my nerves about how I need to take my ass to the states and be with her. I will, but when I'm ready. She's the one who wouldn't allow me to explain shit and won't take my calls. Shit, she better hope I don't make her

wait for me.

Morgan

"Where is he?" I stormed into the spot where they had personal doctors to take care of them.

"He's good sis." Alex said guiding me into a small room.

I was face timing Miguel back and when he didn't answer I instantly knew something was off. Ever since we've gotten back together, he's never allowed my call to go to voicemail. After I left him for those few months, it's as if he made sure to let me know his whereabouts. For those who believe he didn't suffer the way Elaina did; trust me when I say he did. Just because I didn't kill or stab him doesn't mean he got off easy.

I know all about him shutting down on his family because we weren't together. He sent me gifts, called and text me daily, and even stayed in my house for a few days and I still didn't want him. People assume because you give the man a second chance he didn't suffer but mentally and emotionally, he did.

Especially when I had my nervous breakdown. His ass was right by my side. He even cried and begged me to take him back but I couldn't do it. The hurt from him having another child and cheating was too fresh. I can say, those few months of not being around one another, made our love stronger when we did reconnect.

When Alex called me yesterday to tell me something happened to MJ, I lost it. I was hysterical crying and I felt like he wouldn't be alive when I arrived. My mom took me and Le Le to the airport and waited with us. Luckily she was able to calm me down after speaking with his mom. She did mention MJ was shot and in surgery but the doctors were optimistic of him pulling through. They didn't know where or how many times he was hit yet, but the person who did it, was in fact dead.

Now I'm standing here looking over my fiancé who is lying in a hospital bed with tubes in his nose, mouth and monitors on his body. They say he's ok but the sight of him, says different. His moms' eyes were blood shot red and his father had death in his. How in the hell is all of this happening? I moved closer, placed a kiss on his lips and his eyes shot open. He snatched the tube out his mouth and tried to sit up. The monitors were beeping as he snatched them off his chest.

"Where is Camila?" I gave him a crazy look. Why did he wake up looking for some bitch?

"Miguel, I know you're not asking me about a bitch."

"If you think it's another woman, then bounce. I'm tired of telling you there's no one else. Yea, I messed up but if this is what I'm going to deal with, I'll pass." Even though his voice was raspy as hell from the tube he snatched out, the venom was clear.

"Miguel, I'm not saying.-" He cut me off and stood up, only to almost fall. Alex and his dad ran over to catch him.

28

"Get out Morgan and don't bring your ass around me again until you're over the past. I got too much shit going on in my life to pacify the bullshit in your mind." My mouth hit the floor.

"Bro, she doesn't know." Alex said as they helped him back on the bed.

"I know she doesn't and I would've told her, had she asked and not accused me."

"Miguel I'm sorry. What do you expect?"

"I expect you to trust that when I proposed, I meant every word I said. I won't ever cheat on you again and you're all the woman I need." I felt tears falling down my face. I watched his proposal over and over and each time, I would still cry.

"But this shit right here." He pointed between us.

"Tells me you're not over it and will always think I'm cheating. I don't want a insecure woman by my side." I nodded my head, told everyone goodbye and left. He may be in pain but he's not talking to me anyway he wants.

"My daughter better not leave this country." I stopped in my tracks.

"Who said I was leaving?"

"All you do is run back to the states when you get mad. Be my guest and hop on a plane but she's not coming."

"Miguel, if you think I'm leaving her.-"

"Nah. If you think you're leaving with her, you're in for a rude awakening." I could argue with him but I know if he said that, there's no way, I'd get off the estate with her. I opened the door and ran out.

"Morgan, before you think it, he's not shutting you out." His mom said walking behind me.

"Did you hear the way he spoke to me? I don't know about you but it was uncalled for."

"I would agree but then again, he's right." I pulled on the car door. I don't know why I'd assume she'd agree with me.

"Listen. I'll let him tell you who Camila is, but she's not who you think. However, I get why your upset but before you snapped, you should've asked who she was. If it were another woman then you had every right to go off. Morgan honey." She took my hand in hers.

"I've gone through the same shit with his father, unfortunately for me, it was another woman at one point but when I accused him after we moved past it, I was wrong.

"Really." I knew her husband cheated.

"Yup and one day in front of his sister, his bodyguards and the so called woman, I went off. At the time, Miguel had an enemy who sent the woman to accuse him of sleeping with her. Because he had cheated previously, I automatically believed her story. All it did was show his enemy that our marriage wasn't strong. Miguel left me over it." I covered my mouth.

"He told me if I couldn't get over the past, then our future is doomed." I could see the pain on her face as she spoke on it.

"Morgan, you are the first woman he's allowed this close to him and when you left him, he shut down. Yes, he messed up and if you don't want him or can't move past the infidelity, it's best you leave. He won't let you take Le Le, but he will set you up in a house over here and you know you'll always be taken care of."

"I want to marry him and.-"

"Honey you can say it all you want but you have to believe it. He doesn't want to hear his mistake every time you get upset. You have to move past this or I hate to tell you, but you're going to lose him." I nodded my head and stood there listening to her break it down.

I did love Miguel with all my heart but she's right. I have to deal with my inner demons before I can be there for him. I told her Le Le was at their house with Mariana and that I'm going back to the states for a few days. It's not enough time to move past things but it gives me time to be alone and think if this is what I want.

****

"Where is my grandbaby?" My dad asked when I walked in the house.

"With her father." I dropped my bags, ran up the steps, slammed my door and fell on the bed crying. I heard a light knock at the door. I told the person to come in and sat up to wipe my eyes.

"What did he do now?" My father took a seat next to me.

"He woke up asking about a female. I didn't know who she was and accused him of looking for another woman."

"Morgan look." I turned my head towards him.

"I know you love MJ, hell, everyone does but if you can't move past what he did, its best that the two of you co-parent and go your separate ways." Why do I feel like everyone is saying the same thing?

"I know MJ loves me and regrets what he did but how do I move past it?"

"I'm not saying it would be easy but why would you go back if you weren't fully over it. You see, women now a days don't want to see their man with anyone else, so they stick around regardless of the hurt. You kept him away for months and all he did was prove how much he loved you by waiting. Then he proposed and you accepted with no problem. Again, you made him believe you were starting over and forgave him but how could you when you're still accusing him?"

"Dad.-"

"No Morgan. You're wrong this time and I don't care who don't agree with what I'm saying. The bottom line is, you need to leave that man alone and find yourself. This isn't you and I've never seen you broken over a man."

"You think I'm broken?"

"Brokenhearted yes. Broken as in fragile or weak, no."

"I love him and you're right, I don't want him with anyone else but how do I get passed what happened?"

"First off, you have to start seeing someone to deal with your nervous breakdown." I looked at him.

"You stayed in the hospital for a few days but you never took the woman up on her offer to come in. What you went through needs to be dealt with, then that little stay you had in the hospital." I didn't like the way he said that and he must've known.

"Look. I know its hard facing the truth but honey you have to love yourself before you can love him and even Le Le for that matter."

"I love my daughter."

"Morgan, he's not saying you don't." My mom said coming it the room. I didn't realize she heard or knew we were talking.

"Well it sounds that way to me." I caught an attitude.

"All he's saying is, your life will be better when you love yourself again. You were so busy giving it all to him and your daughter that you forgot about yourself. The nervous breakdown you had, was telling your body to relax. Maybe Le Le being with her dad will give you the time you need to get back to your old self. You know he won't dare allow anything to happen to her, so before you say it, don't. Get your head right and then go get your family back." I busted out crying and my mom came to sit on the other side of me.

"I just want to be happy like we were in the beginning. I know he loves me but how could he sleep with her and.-"

"Morgan, leave it in the past."

"I don't know how?"

"Ask your mom how she did it." My dad said and stood up.

"Bruno."

"I'm serious Melina. I don't like seeing my daughter cry and I did you the same way a few times." My mom sucked her teeth.

"I'm not proud of it but it did happen. Teach her how to get through it but I'm telling you now Morgan. If you do get past it, don't bring it up again. He's not the type of man who will continue to let you badger him over it." I nodded my head. He kissed me and let me and my mom talk. I wiped my eyes and asked her how did she do it.

"Oh girl please. I had sex with someone else." I covered my mouth.

"What?" She shrugged her shoulders like what she said was ok.

"Shit, I may not have cheated on him, but knowing I slept with another man, fixed his ass right up. That man wouldn't let me out of his sight after that."

"What do you mean you didn't cheat? But you slept with someone else."

"I slept with someone else when we broke up."

"Should I sleep with someone else?"

"Morgan I would never tell you to do that. Don't get me wrong, it would definitely make it even and give him some shit to think about. However, that nigga MJ, ain't nothing to fuck with." I laughed when she said that.

"I'm serious. These generations of kids are nothing like when we were coming up. If you even entertained another man, I think he would have sex with you one last time before he killed you." We both started laughing. Everyone told me I better not be with another man, and as bad as I want to, just to get him back, I can't because then I'd be as bad as him.

"Thanks ma."

"Anytime baby. I do want you to speak to someone about the breakdown. You may be fine now but it can happen again. I also don't want you slipping into depression. Lord knows if you go back in the hospital, your baby father will flip on the staff again."

When I was in the hospital they tried to place me on the crazy floor and Miguel flipped out so bad, they gave me a private room on a different floor, at the end of the hall. Since he refused to leave, the doctors and nurses were petrified to come in. I swear I loved him but my parents are right about me learning to love myself again. Le Le was fine where she was and I can only hope Miguel can handle her because she is a

piece of work.

Aiden

"Ride it just like that baby." I stared at Joy rocking back and forth on top of me.

She was indeed a beautiful woman and I needed to thank her parents a lot more for having her. Not just for her looks but everything that comes with her. She's going to have my baby soon, she's a good person despite what went down with my sister, and her pussy has a hold on my dick. I ain't never had a woman who could hold my attention the way she does. I'm not even interested in being with anyone else since she's been in my life.

She is close to six and a half months and I refused to let her travel a lot. For the time being she's been staying with me. Her father wasn't too happy about it, but he told me as long as her security was there, he felt safe. Of course, he sat me down and threatened me and my family's life if anything happened to her. I understood and didn't take offense to it because I'd be doing the same when my daughter comes. No we don't know what we're having yet, but I'm just saying.

"AJ, I'm... getting ready... to cummmmmm. She moaned out and laid on my chest. I wasn't through with her though. I placed her on her back, lifted her legs on my shoulder and dug as deep as I could. It took some time for her to get used to me and now that she is. I'm telling you, she's my own personal pornstar.

"You wet as fuck baby." Her juices were making a lot of noise and it was driving me insane. I couldn't hold out anymore and came inside her. I fell on the side of her and wrapped my arm around her stomach. I felt the baby move and smiled. My kid was active as hell in her belly and I couldn't wait to meet him or her.

"Baby, your mom and aunt are coming in an hour to take me to the store. She wants to buy the crib and some other things."

"Dammit Joy. I told you to say we didn't need anything." She sat up.

"AJ don't make me fuck you up. If you didn't want anything, then you tell her. You're not putting me on their bad side. Always talking about tell my mom and aunt this or that. I don't see you saying shit. Trying to get them to yell at me. Nigga shit." She tossed the covers back and walked in the bathroom naked, talking more shit in Spanish. I couldn't help but laugh and get turned on when she spoke. I went in the bathroom and stood there watching her silhouette through the glass door.

"Stop staring at me like a creep." She must've felt my presence because I didn't say a word.

"Oh I'm a creep." I pulled the glass open further and stepped in. I rubbed her stomach and then kissed it.

"Are you happy with me Aiden?"

"Joy, don't ask me again."

"I want to be sure that you're with me for the right reasons."

"First off... I'm with you because I am in love with you. Second... your family may have more money than me but I'm no broke nigga. And third... what's in between your legs has a nigga strung out. I don't know if it's because I'm your first or that you're my personal freak. Whatever the case; I'm yours only. Listen." I made her look at me.

"I know my baby has your hormones going crazy but I'm going to be here. Plus, I'm your first and last sex partner. So don't even think about trying to leave me to venture on the other side." She smacked me on my arm.

"I don't want anyone else AJ. I see how my brother did Morgan and I don't want to be her. We all know MJ loves her but it wasn't enough when he cheated."

"Men fuck up Joy and if I'm playing devils advocate; she did send him a message saying she was leaving him and he needed to stay away from her. Technically she broke up with him."

"He didn't have to.-" I cut her off.

"You're right; he didn't but shorty caught him in a drunken state and used it to her advantage. He could've stopped it and didn't but it is what it is."

"But.-"

"But nothing. That's their business and I'm not about to get into a debate with you over it and you end up mad at me all day. You start holding out on the pussy and I'm not trying to hear it." I placed some kisses on her lips and neck and continued washing up. Joy loved her brothers and I'm sure it hurt her to see them upset or going through something but she's not about to take me through it.

After we got out the shower and put our clothes on, we went downstairs to eat. I grabbed my cell off the kitchen counter and noticed Akeem was calling me. I picked it up and he asked me to meet him at PJ's house, which is weird as hell. When I asked why, he told me Zariah went to get his son and that her parents were on their way to the house too. He felt something wasn't right and wanted to make sure.

See Akeem isn't a punk but he does try to stay out of bullshit. However, if anyone messed with his family or Zariah, he turned into another person. I hung up and told Joy to wait for my mom and aunt and that I'd see her later.

I hopped in the car and hit DJ up, who in return, hit James Jr. and everyone else. When I pulled up big Dayquan had PJ's mom yoked up and Zariah was on the ground. None of us asked questions and started hooking off on all the niggas standing out there.

All of a sudden we heard gunshots. Everyone stopped and I saw Akeem's body hit the ground. Tara still had the gun pointing at him with a smile on her face. I ran over to him and blood was gushing out. We got him in the car and sped all the way to the hospital.

"AJ, your mom is getting on my nerves." My aunt said when she answered the phone. She sounded so happy and here I am calling her with bad news.

"Aunt Phoenix, get to the hospital."

"What? AJ, I can't hear you." I repeated myself and she started panicking.

My mom took the phone from her and I told her the same thing without telling it all. I hung up and yelled for DJ to hurry up. He was driving my car as I sat in the back trying to keep Akeem conscious by talking.

DJ jumped out and ran inside once we pulled up at the ER. James Jr. and Darius came rushing to the car and helped me carry him in. The doctors and nurses came running and had us place him on the stretcher. I looked down at myself and saw blood over my clothes.

"What happened to him?" I heard and turned to see DJ's mom coming towards us. We began telling her and that's when we found out Zariah passed out, hit her head real hard and was unconscious.

"WHERES'S MY SON?" My uncle, my aunt, Joy and my parents came rushing in.

"They have him in the back. Unc, Tara shot him a few times but I don't know where. It was a lot of blood so I can't tell you how many hit him."

"What the fuck did she shoot him for and does anyone have her? Where the fuck is she?" My uncle was fuming and pacing.

My aunt fell on the chair and laid her head on my mom's shoulder. I had Joy take a seat because she looked tired. A few minutes later, Gabby and Brea came in. I gave each of them a hug and sat next to my sister. Her and Joy were cordial but as far a being best buddies, I doubt that would happen anytime soon.

"You ok baby." I asked when I walked over to her. I kept checking on her too.

"Yea. I'm hungry though. I'm going to walk to the cafeteria to find something to eat. Do you want anything?"

"Nah, I'm good."

"Does anyone else want something."

"I do. Can you get me a sandwich and fries if they have it? Also." Gabby ran a list down to Joy and I had to stop her.

"Gabby, she's just getting a little and you're ordering a damn meal for all of us."

"I'm hungry too AJ."

"Well go with her then." She rolled her eyes.

"My girl is not walking back with all that shit because you want to be lazy. Take your greedy as with her and Brea too. I swear you better not come back with mad shit either." Gabby stuck her finger up and had Brea take a walk with her and Joy.

"Does it look bad?" My dad and uncle sat next to me on both sides.

"Honestly, I can't say. It was a lot of blood but I don't know how many times he got hit. I wish I could tell you more." I had my head down wiping the lone tear that fell.

"I'm going to kill her and her fucked up family." My uncle said hopping out of his seat. It didn't even dawn on me at the time to snatch Tara's ass up. I was so worried about my cousin that she was able to get away.

"Steel please. Don't leave right now. I need you here." My aunt Phoenix said and he stopped in his tracks. He went over and stood her in front of him.

"He's going to be fine baby."

"You think so. Steel, I can't lose my son."

"Phoenix, I promise you, we won't." They walked to the nurses' station and asked again if there was any news yet and a doctor came out at the same time. I looked down at my

50

clock and noticed a half hour passed and the girls still weren't back. I called Joy's phone and no one answered and the same with my sister and cousin. She did send me a text to ask if I were hungry again.

"Hi, I'm doctor Wheeler." He shook their hands and we all stood by them.

"Your son is still in surgery but I'm here to give you a rundown of what's going on thus far." He said and we waited for him to speak. He guided us in another room first but I made them keep the door open in case the girls came back.

"As of right now we've found three bullets in your son's stomach and one in his arm. Unfortunately, the three in his stomach were in different areas and the doctor's are still struggling to remove them." My aunt gasped.

"He has lost a tremendous amount of blood and we had to give him at least three transfusions already. He has a huge knot on the back of his head that has us concerned because there's also a huge gash in it." I shrugged my shoulders.

"The other doctor is doing his best to remove the bullets, however, if we can't get one out, do we have your permission to leave it in thee until a later time? The reason I ask is because in certain situations it may be better to leave it in and deal with it later, because it may actually hurt him to take it out."

"Its fine. Do whatever you need to do, to keep my son alive. Please don't let him die." My aunt was hysterical speaking but made sure she was clear when saying that.

"I can assure you, he is in the best hands right now." He went to leave.

"Oh, I almost forgot. After the surgery, he will be placed in ICU." No one said a word as we all watched the doctor walk away.

"See. He's going to be fine Phoenix. We just have to wait for them to finish." I stepped out the room and called Joy again. I bet their greedy asses stayed in the cafeteria to eat. I sat down with everyone else waiting and praying for the best.

Joy

I was a tad bit uncomfortable going to the cafeteria with Gabby and Brea. Not because I feared them, but more so because we weren't really fucking with each other like that. Yea, Gabby and I spoke and were cordial but we didn't call each other on the phone or hang out either.

People think when you're in a relationship with a guy, you're in one with the family and that's far from the truth. When you befriend some families they become emotionally involved as well and cause more damage. In my opinion it's better to be cool with them from a distance. What he and I go through is between us. I'm the type of bitch who's like, just because I'm with someone in your family, we don't have to be friends.

As we stepped off the elevator I noticed a slight pudge in Brea's belly. She and I were definitely cool being she's with my cousin Mateo. She did however stop speaking to me after the incident with Gabby but over time, we managed to get to where we used to be.

I stopped walking and asked if she was pregnant and Gabby looked at her. Once she said yes, we all got real excited. It seemed as if we would be raising our kids together and none of us could wait.

I picked a tray up and walked inside the cafeteria looking at what they had. It was cold sandwiches and they also had a grill to make hot food on. My stomach grumbled when a man passed us with a fresh cheeseburger and hot fries. All of us basically ran to the grill and placed an order. I sent a text AJ to see if he was hungry but he didn't answer. I figured they were all smoking outside as usual.

After our food was done, we sat down and all of us had to be hungry because we were finished in no time. I stood to empty my tray and felt a slight bump on my arm. The person said excuse me so I paid it no mind.

Gabby asked me if I were ok and I didn't know why until she said who the person was. We followed behind Shayla and met her at the elevators. She sucked her teeth when she noticed us but covered her mouth when she saw my belly.

"Why did you bump me?"

"I didn't know it was you. If you'll excuse me, I need to get to my son."

"Your son." Gabby asked with her face turned up.

"Yes my son and before you ask, yes AJ knows. He came up here yesterday when I had him." I was flabbergasted when she revealed that but refused to allow her to see me upset. AJ said he had some running around to do but failed to mention she was involved.

"And." Gabby was rude as hell.

"And he took a test and it came back earlier today. I hate to tell you this but it's his baby." I wanted to punch her in the face. Not because she had a baby by him but how she went about it.

"Well I want to see him then." Gabby said when the elevator doors finally opened for us to get on.

"Go ahead. He's in the nursery. I only came down to get some food because the hospital food is disgusting."

"Did we ask you why you were here? Just show us the baby." Brea said in a disappointing tone.

The elevator stopped on the fourth floor and I felt my phone going off. Of course, it was AJ so I ignored it. Gabby's went off next and then Brea's but like me, they ignored it too. We went to the nursery and they said the baby wasn't there. When we got to her room an older woman was holding him.

"Who are they?" She asked Shayla and handed her the baby.

"This is AJ's sister." She pointed to Gabby.

"This is his cousin." She pointed to Brea.

"And this is. I'm sorry who are you again." Shayla was trying to be smart but I had a trick for her ass.

"I am his woman. You know the one you tried to keep away with your lies."

"Excuse me." Her mom said and stood up.

"You heard her. Your daughter did some scandalous shit because he didn't want to be with her. I don't know why she's sitting over there pretending to be perfect." I smiled listening to Gabby have my back.

"Shayla what are they speaking about? I thought you and AJ were together." I busted out laughing. This bitch is delusional as hell, telling her mom that.

"Ooooh let me tell it ladies. Its really a funny story and I would love to see her moms face."

"GET OUT!" Shayla screamed and woke the baby up. I ignored her and continued speaking.

"My man AJ used to fuck your daughter." Her mom turned her face up but oh well.

"Yea and when we got together he left her alone. Matter of fact, He sent her tons of messages telling her it was over but she wasn't trying to hear it. AJ came to see me in Puerto Rico and we were in a bad accident. She came over with his family, never informing them that they were no longer a couple, not that they ever were one.

Long story short, AJ was in a coma and your daughter hopped on his dick. He woke up in the process and since he was hard, he made her suck it. Instead of swallowing his seeds, Miss Shayla here, jumped back on his dick and had him cum inside her."

"Stop lying Joy. He was awake." I moved over to where she was.

"He was awake but you knew he had no strength after being in a coma for two months. You took advantage of him and should be ashamed of yourself on how this baby got here."

"Shayla, is that true?"

"Ma."

"SHAYLA! Is it true?" Shayla put her head down.

"That's fucking disgusting. Shayla, I know damn well I raised you better than that. You fucked a man at his weakest moment and then had his baby. Did he even want this child?" I folded my arms and waited for her to answer.

"No. When she came to tell him, he slammed the door in her face." Shayla broke down crying and I had the biggest smile on my face. She was so busy trying to hurt me because she had his kid that it backfired. *Stupid bitch!*

"What the hell are y'all doing in here?" We heard AJ bark as he came in the room.

"The question isn't why we're here, but why are you?"

"My son's mother sent me a text that y'all were in here ganging up on her. Why she crying? What the fuck Gabby? Joy, I know you didn't put your hands on her." Me, Brea and Gabby all stood there with our mouths opened.

"They came in here talking shit and made me wake the baby up. AJ, I thought they were going to jump me with little Aiden." My head snapped towards him.

"Hold on Joy." He tried to grab my hand.

"You told me our son would be a junior. Are you serious?"

"Baby, she had my son first and.-"

"You knew it was a possibility. Did you sign the birth certificate with his name on it?" He didn't answer.

"DID YOU?"

"What does it matter if I did?"

"It matters because everything you said was a lie. Just like you told me yesterday you had running around to do but you were here. Let me guess, it slipped your mind right?"

"I only stayed for two hours." I scoffed up a laugh and headed towards the door. Now it was time for the bitch to have a big ass smile on her face.

"You know what AJ. We are done, finished, over."

"Good. He didn't want you anyway. If he did, he could've pushed me off but instead, he came in me willingly." Shayla yelled and AJ had an evil look on his face as if he wanted to kill her.

"Good thing, I don't want him anymore either. AJ, enjoy your time with the baby."

"He will, you stupid bitch. I had his first son and he's a junior. You thought you were better than me but you're not. If you were, he wouldn't have hid the fact he came here or named his son after him." She threw her head back laughing. I ran over and punched her in the face so hard, her nose bled instantly.

"Joy, you're pregnant." AJ pulled me off her.

"Oh now, its' Joy you're pregnant. AJ, you're a fucking joke. I'm telling you right now in front of her and your son that I don't ever want to see you again. When I have the baby, I'll make arrangements for you to be with him. I mean, its not like it'll matter being you have a son already."

"I wish you would leave." He shouted.

"Oh, you know better than to threaten me."

"And you know, I'm not scared of shit."

"I know, which is going to make watching you suffer, even better." He tried to jump in front of me but Brea pushed him out the way.

"AJ, you stay messing up. You never should've allowed that bitch to speak to Joy anyway she wanted." I heard Gabby say as we were at the elevators waiting.

"Then you come up in the room automatically blaming Joy. The bitch told us to come up there. Shayla knew exactly what she was doing and your stupid ass fell for it. I'm sorry bro, but I'm with Joy on this. I hope she never comes back to you."

"Really sis."

"I'm serious AJ. She is pregnant and you got this bitch talking out the side of her neck, with you standing right there. Joy was your woman and you were supposed to have her back, not some bitch who got pregnant on purpose." I stepped on the elevator wiping my eyes. I couldn't believe after everything we had gone through, it came down to this. The doors closed with him yelling out my name.

"Is everything ok?" Arizona asked as soon as she saw me.

"I'm ok. I'll see you later."

"What's the matter Joy?" His father asked.

"I just need to lay down. I'm tired and.-"

"I'll fill them in Joy, don't worry. Do what you have to?" Gabby gave me a hug and I walked to the Uber Brea called for me.

"Joy! Joy!" I turned around and AJ was running to me. I asked the driver to take me straight to the airport.

I only had clothes at his house so there was no need for me to go there. My phone began to ring off the hook from him. I called my dad and told him I was going to Teterboro airport and hopping a flight home. If I went to Newark, I'm sure AJ would catch me there.

"I'll see you when you get here." My dad said before hanging up.

The Uber parked in front of the airport. I stepped out and my security was in a different truck. I could've rode with them but I wanted to be alone. After an hour it was time for me to get on the plane. AJ had a lot of growing up to do and he had to start with learning how to stop lying. If not, we'd never be together again.

Zariah

"Are you ok baby?" I heard my mom asking in my ear. I opened my eyes and noticed my head was in my moms lap. I heard yelling, people cursing and turned a little to see pure chaos around me.

"What's going on?" I felt someone helping me up.

"You and your mom need to leave." He was carrying me and running to the car.

"Akeem. When did you get here?"

"Mrs. Martin can you take her to the hospital and I'll be there shortly?"

"Akeem, what's going on?"

"Zariah just go. We'll talk later." He helped me in and my mom ran on the drivers' side. I looked back in the yard and my dad hit some guy so hard, he was laid out. Then I saw AJ,

Akeem, DJ, James Jr. and everyone else I'm related to, laying

niggas out.

POP! POP! POP! POP! Is all I heard next, and my

mom sped off.

"Ma, we have to go back." I pulled the mirror down

and looked at my face.

"Zariah you need a doctor." She pointed to a big ass

knot on the side of my temple.

"I'm fine. Turn around."

"No. You passed out and hit your head."

"I feel fine." As I said that, my stomach became queasy

and it felt like I needed to vomit. I had her pull over and

emptied the contents in my stomach. My head became dizzy

again and then it was black.

****

67

"She'll be fine. When she hit her head, it caused her to have a concussion, which is why she threw up and blacked out. However, the reason she passed out in the first place, is because she's pregnant and extremely dehydrated." The doctor said.

I had opened my eyes but never informed anyone I was awake. Once the doctor told them I was pregnant, my hands went straight to my stomach and that's when my dad ran over to me.

"You good." He kissed my forehead and grabbed my hand.

The look on his face wasn't a good one, which told me something was wrong. I glanced around the room to see everyone there except AJ and Aiden. I didn't even see Brea, who is my best friend. I did think Gabby would be here too, but in her state she probably stayed home.

"Where's Akeem? He's going to be so happy." I smiled and propped myself up on the bed the best I could.

"Ummmm sweetie. Maybe you should get some more rest. You hit your head really hard." My mom said and laid in the bed with me.

"Please don't tell me he had another damn kid or he's with another woman. I swear to God if that's the case, I'm killing him."

"Shut your ass up." DJ came over to me and sat on the edge.

"Tara shot Akeem and he's in surgery. They don't know if he's going to make it." And just like that I passed the hell out again.

I'm starting to believe no one wants me to be happy. I mean Akeem has been getting Jacob on a regular now; well I've been picking him up but he's spending time with him. He still gives her money and there's no verbal connection in any way. Why in the hell did she shoot him? It had to be because he doesn't want her, but she has or had CJ and is pregnant by him.

I don't know how long I was out but when I woke up, my dad was the only one in the room. He came over to me when he noticed me awake and asked if I needed anything. My dad looked stressed out. It doesn't look like he's slept in days and the lines on his forehead showed aggravation.

I asked him to help me up so I could go in the bathroom. My head still hurt and I wanted to take a shower. As I was using the toilet, there was a knock on the door. It was the nurse coming in to assist me. I guess they didn't want me to fall again.

"Where's mommy?" I asked when I finished.

"Your mom isn't speaking to me right now."

"What happened?"

"When that stupid bitch Candy brought up the past, your mom got in her feelings and flipped on me. She blames me for her bringing up old memories. I don't know Zariah. I'm not going to lie and say I didn't take your mom through a lot because I did. However, I thought we moved past it after all these years but I guess your mom didn't. She won't speak to me and has been staying with your aunt Mariah."

"Have you been home to talk about it?"

"I go home to change and come up here with you. You, your mom and my sons are my main concern, not some bullshit from the past she claimed to be over. I love your mom and if she wants to be mad, then so be it. I'm not reliving and dealing with the shit again." He shrugged his shoulders. I have to agree with him though. My mom should be ashamed of herself, being that happened over twenty years ago.

"I'm sorry dad. I still love you and I don't hold any animosity towards you. What happened in the past is that, the past. I'm surprised to know Tara and PJ are my cousins but you didn't even know, so how could I be mad?"

"Man, I had no idea they were even living here. She was in Georgia back then. It makes me wonder what her purpose was for coming to Jersey. Think about it Zariah. After all these years we've never heard about them. All of a sudden they pop up. From what you say, Tara never liked you, which is why she got pregnant by Akeem. Then her brother PJ has a relationship with Gabby, only to abuse her the same way his dad did your mom and his. Come to find out, he's working with whoever this is trying to bring your cousin down. All of it is connected and until we find out who this chick is, we won't know." I thought about what he said, and it made a lot of sense.

In the last two years it's as if someone was trying to tear us apart. Instead of going after our parents, they're coming for us. What I want to know is why not end the beef with who it started with?

The nurse came in to check my vitals and I asked if she could find out about Akeem. She told me he was in ICU but that she'd take me to see him if I wanted. My dad said he was coming with us because he couldn't take the chance of anything else happening.

When we got off the floor, the nurse pushed the wheelchair to the nurses' station. After she spoke to them for a minute, she pushed me in his room. No one was in there and that alone had me concerned. Tara could come up anytime or even send someone up to finish him off and I wasn't having that. The nurse and my dad left me in the room with him alone. You could see them talking through the glass window.

"Akeem baby. I need you to wake up. I have something to tell you." The nurse said he was heavily medicated due to being shot. She didn't go in to detail about how much damage was done and right now, I wasn't sure I was ready to hear it anyway.

"I'm going to make sure Tara gets what she has coming to her. She won't get away with this." All you could hear were the monitors beeping and the blood pressure cuff going off. I kissed his hand and laid my head on the bed. I wanted to lie next to him but it was impossible. I was scared I'd move him the wrong way and something happen. I needed him to wake up and not be in more pain than he's already in. I waved my hand for my dad to come in.

"Dad, we can't leave him unattended. I mean, what if she comes back?"

"His dad is on his way up here. His parents went home to change and told the nurses no one was allowed to see him but you. You see that man right there?" He pointed to some white guy who was reading a magazine.

"Yea."

"He's here watching over Akeem. His dad made sure to make him incognito just in case."

"Makes sense."

"Yea, he had to take Akeem's mom home to rest. She isn't doing good."

"I have to call her."

"Yea, I think she'll be happy to hear from you. She kept asking about you too. But since you're here, you two will see each other." I nodded my head. He pulled a seat up and sat next to me. I loved my dad and whatever mistakes he made in the past, should stay there. I had some words for my mom because this shit is petty as hell, if you ask me.

Right now, I'm going to pray Akeem gets up before I go to my room but if not, I'll be here everyday until he does.

CJ

I know a lot of you assumed a nigga was dead when you read I pulled the trigger. Funny thing about that is, there were no bullets in the gun.

"Wait!" I heard my sister Patience yell. Her and my brother both gave me a hug. I closed my eyes and pulled the trigger.

Click! After seeing nothing happened, I pulled it again.

"Doesn't matter how many times you try, nothing's going to happen." MJ said smirking.

"I see you were going out like a G but I promised CiCi, I wouldn't take you from her and I don't, well let's say, I try not to break promises." He moved closer.

His security sat me down in a chair and placed my hand on the table. MJ walked up, pulled a knife out his pocket and stuck it straight in my hand like Nino Brown did the guy in

New Jack City. The pain was excruciating and I didn't care what anyone thought, I had to scream.

"Never bite the hand that would have fed you cousin." I had tears rolling down my eyes as MJ poured acid on my entire left hand.

"Yo that shit is nasty." James Jr. said and moved back because he was gagging.

"Do you know why I did that to your hands?"

"No." My words were slurring as I listened to him go in on me.

"I poured acid on the right hand because it's the one you held the gun up to your sisters head with. You were stabbed in your other hand to remind you how you went against family. You know as well as anyone, that disrespect, betrayal, backstabbing and being deceitful is not tolerated." I didn't say a word. I should've never listened to Denise.

"Here's what's going to happen though." I felt a pinch in my neck and instantly fell out the chair and to the ground.

My body felt as if it were shutting down. All of a sudden my lower half had a weird sensation. You know the feeling when your foot falls asleep; it was the same. Darius came closer to me pushing a wheelchair. It wasn't a regular wheelchair either. It was the kind that had the neckpiece to it, along with straps. Security helped me get in the chair and soon after, my entire body was numb.

"I injected you with a serum that will have you temporarily paralyzed. I did this because, well to be honest, it was this or death." He thought the shit was funny but then again, he was a crazy motherfucker and I underestimated him.

"From now on, you will need someone to take care of you until I'm ready to have it reversed. You will need to be changed, fed, bathed and whatever else is needed for the time being." Again I couldn't say anything.

"You will live with your parents and I suggest you pray, my dear cousin, that your father doesn't beat your ass while you're laid up, after all the shit you put CiCi through. I will never understand how a person can be so damn disrespectful to a woman who raised him. She beat Denise's ass for abusing you and made sure you had the best of everything. If that were me, I'd be kissing the ground she walked on everyday and sending her on thousands of vacations." He backed up and handed a bag to James Jr.

"This is all the money he had in the safes at his two homes. His houses were cleaned out and will be sold as well. CiCi can do whatever she wants with it. " James nodded and MJ started to walk away.

"I took everything from you nigga, because you tried to take it from me. Cousin or not, if and when I decide to give you the freedom to move again, and you try to come for me; you're dead on sight and so is that bastard baby Tara has in her stomach." Oh shit! How did he know about her?

Patience put the straps around me and all of a sudden some big buff dude came strolling in with an EMT shirt on. He had a medical bag, opened it and began to wrap my hand up. Blood was everywhere and I could hear my brother still gagging. After he had me wrapped up, he pushed me out the door and rolled me onto some ramp that is connected to a van. If I never felt what is what like to be handicapped, I do now.

The next destination was to the hospital where they put me to sleep to handle both of my hands. By the time I woke up, I had stitches in one hand and half of my arm was gone on the other. Evidently, gangrene and infection set in right away and they had to remove from my elbow down. My life was shitty right now and the only person to blame is me.

"You did this to yourself CJ." My mom said holding the cup to my mouth for me to drink.

"I know ma." She moved the cup from my mouth, picked the fork up and began feeding me a piece of steak. Of course my food had to be cut up like a damn baby but hey, I'm alive to eat so I wasn't complaining.

"You think I'm a bad person?" She wiped my mouth and took a seat next to me.

"CJ, I think you were so caught up in trying to have your birth mother love you, that you forgot who was there for you. Honey, your mom was obsessed over your dad and trust me when I say, I know why." She laughed.

"Ma really. I do not need to know how dad.- Yuk! Just forget it." She tossed her head back laughing harder.

"Anyway, she has always wanted a life with your father. He's told her time and time again, it would never happen. CJ, before he met me, he never wanted a relationship with her. Not only that, she kept him away from you for all those years. She knew he didn't want any kids with anyone but his wife, who he didn't have yet. But your mom kept you and used you, to try and get him back on more than one occasion."

"Did my father want me?"

"He didn't know about you. I swear when your mom friend requested me on social media; it was for me to see you. She thought I'd leave your dad and he'd run to her. However, what they shared was before my time and I'd never take it out on you. I loved you as my own, the moment I laid eyes on you. You may think I didn't love you the same way I did with your siblings but I never thought twice about treating you different. You were and still are my son." I felt the tears coming down my face and she used her hands to wipe them. I did my family wrong for a woman who used me as a pawn in her game.

"I'm sorry for everything ma."

"I know baby and so does everyone else."

"Dad probably hates me."

"He doesn't hate you CJ. He hates what you did but once he found out why you did it, he understood. However, he'll never be ok with you putting hands on me or disrespecting me or any other woman."

"I didn't mean to do that. It was a reflex but I know better." She nodded her head and smiled. I could see why my father was head over heels in love with her. What's not to love?

"Excuse me Mrs. Thomas. It's time for his bath." The nurse Connie said. My mom wiped the few tears she let fall, kissed my cheek and took my plate and cup off the table.

"I'll be back son. And you better not let me catch you trying to get his dick hard again." Connie put her head down.

I had to laugh because the other day I wanted to see if I could get aroused and asked her to try. My mom walked in to ask me something and went the fuck off. She probably thought the nurse was trying to rape me but it wasn't the case.

"I told you she's still mad." Connie said and began to put me in the Hoyer lift. For those of you that aren't aware of what it is. It's a device that handicap people use to get lifted and transported from one spot to another. I really only use it to get in the tub. I have a seat in there with straps I sit in, as she bathes me. I'll be damned if I'm handicapped and dirty.

After she washed me and put my clothes on, she sat next to me like always and we indulged in movies on Netflix. She was my seven pm to seven am nurse; and in the morning someone would relieve her. Fortunately for me, she and I talked a lot about any and everything.

I know MJ was teaching me a lesson but with each day passing I wanted to get up on my own. I wanted to take Connie out and show her a good time. Especially since she just got finished with nursing school.

The day she graduated her ass came straight here, jumping up and down like a kid on her birthday. Her nametag now had RN on it and she was ecstatic. I had my mom buy her a Pandora bracelet with two nurse charms on it and a few pair of sneakers and clothes. She still lived at home with her mom and nursing school doesn't pay you. I felt it would be nice to see her smile.

"What you thinking about CJ?" She asked after cleaning my catheter bag. Yea, I had to wear one because I had no feeling down there and kept using the bathroom on myself. I swear being handicapped is hard and I wouldn't wish this life on anyone.

"How one day I hope to take you out."

"CJ, I keep telling you that I don't mind going out with you now."

"I would never take you anywhere and I can't move. How am I supposed to open a door for you? Or how can I make love to you after?-" I stopped and stared at her. Who was I fooling? MJ won't ever allow me to move again. It's already been five months and not once has anyone bought up anything. Connie was a gorgeous woman and could have any man she wanted. I would be crazy to think she'd sit around waiting on me.

"CJ, stop it. I know you want to get up but it takes time. When your body is ready, you'll know." I never explained what my cousin did. All she knew was I had been in an accident and was paralyzed, temporarily. She leaned in to kiss me and I turned my head but she turned it back. The way she kissed me made me think, she had the same feelings I did.

"I love you CJ and this doesn't define you." She pointed to my body. I guess she does but this is the first time hearing her say it.

"How can you love me and I'm like this?"

"Easy. In the beginning you were a jerk and an asshole. I hated to come here everyday, however, as the days passed, I saw a different person revealing himself. You let down your guard and let me love you mentally and emotionally. Baby, sex isn't everything and you feasted on me a few times to let me know what your mouth does. In return, I used my toys to satisfy the other part."

I laughed because a few times when no one was here, I had her lay me back on the bed and sit on my face. Now I may not be able to move my body but it ain't a damn thing wrong with my mouth. If my mom knew that she'd probably fire her.

She got in bed beside me and laid there. I couldn't feel her but knowing she's there is enough. I'm having my mom contact MJ tomorrow. I wanted to be with Connie and if I had to beg for MJ's forgiveness for him to reverse this shit, it is what it is.

Akeena

"How am I supposed to take the Rodriquez family down now that CJ is dead?" I asked Armond as we laid in the bed after sex.

"We'll find a different way. Shit, we can probably use Zariah since she's not too happy about finding out we're related."

"How would we do that? It's not like she speaks to your brother and she hates your sister."

"Yea but she doesn't know me." I smirked thinking about how fun it would be to kill Zariah. Armond may not be like PJ as far as being a woman beater but he had his nasty ways too.

"Hell no." Armond doesn't really do violence unless its necessary and I refused to get him caught up and lose his life.

"Relax Akeena. She is my blood cousin and I'm not talking about my cousin who is related by my seventh aunt, whose uncle married their fifth grandmother." I gave him a crazy look. I knew he wouldn't try and sleep with her.

"What? It's possible. Shit, incest runs rampant now a days." He shrugged his shoulders and sat up with his feet hanging. I couldn't do shit but laugh at his ignorance.

"All I'm saying is, no one knows what I look like. We can come up with a plan and once I get her alone, hold her for ransom or some shit. Alex and Zariah are supposedly close, so if MJ doesn't rescue her, he definitely will."

"What about the Gabby chick?"

"Her father isn't letting her out of his sight. Since she lost the first baby, he's making sure nothing happens. It's a lost cause when it comes to her. It's going to be really hard to catch any of them slipping now." I nodded my head and hopped in the shower with him. Neither of us spoke and washed up in our own thoughts. I couldn't help but reminisce on how I got here.

"Same time next week?" The guy asked as I put my clothes on. At the time I didn't know who this guy was but he'd request me every time he came.

It all started with my father having an outside child. His other son Akeem and his brother Aiden came to Africa to take over. Aiden disrespected my father and it was nothing but problems from there.

Miguel Sr. killed my two brothers over his bitch ass wife Violet, which is why my dad even made the attempt for his other son to take his place. He was getting old and knew he wouldn't be able to fight big Miguel.

Once Akeem came aboard, he wanted him to take the Rodriquez clan out. Unbeknownst to my father, Miguel Sr. was Akeem's Connect and he had no intentions of getting involved in my fathers shit. You can read all about it, in the Shawty down to ride for a boss series.

Anyway, my mother tried to have Aiden's wife Arizona thrown in some human trafficking ring they ran. The shit backfired because Aiden came for his wife and what do you know? We ended up taking Arizona's spot.

The man, who we went to, raped and beat us for weeks. Once he finished, he left us alone to get better and began selling us to whomever. One time a man paid twenty dollars to have sex with me and I had to perform every sexual act possible. I was pissed he got all that, for the little bit of money.

Two years ago, Armond and his boys came to have a good time. I showed his ass so much of a good time, he became a regular. Eventually, he killed the guy I was with for whatever reason and we've been together ever since.

Unfortunately, my mother didn't make it out alive. The last appointment she went on, the man killed her for biting his dick. Now I'm here with this perfect man, trying to figure out in my mind if he's really here for me or because he wants to get rid of the Rodriquez clan too.

You may ask why I want the Rodriquez clan when it's clear Arizona and Aiden are the reasons why I ended up where

I did. The way I see it is, if Miguel Sr. never killed my brothers, my father would've never sent for Akeem and we wouldn't be in this mess.

Oh but don't get it twisted; I'm making sure their family suffers too. The accident Gabby was in, is all me and thanks to PJ, he kept her there long enough to make sure the person would get to her. It's a damn shame she didn't die but from what I hear, her father doesn't believe it was an accident. At least he's paying attention.

I still haven't found my son either. Last I heard, he was in a gang and I can pretty much bet, he's probably dead. The gangs over here in Africa are deadly and they don't take any prisoners. I did ask around for him but no one knew who he was or they weren't telling. I did have one person tell me the gang they assumed he was in but when I went asking questions, two dudes pulled a gun out on me, so I left it alone. If he wants to be found, he can look me up.

"You ok?" Armond asked shutting the shower off and wrapping a towel around me.

"Yea. Why?"

"Because I left you in here ten minutes ago and you're still in here. The water is freezing and you were zoned out." I loved how he catered to me.

"I'm good baby. I was just thinking of how we met and how you've been a blessing ever since."

"Well don't think too hard because I'm not going anywhere. Lets get you out of here and dressed. We have some things to do and it starts off with leaving this house to get fresh air." I swear I loved him. Why couldn't we have met prior to how he found me?

****

"So you think a nigga wouldn't find you?" I heard when I answered my phone. Armond was lying next to me knocked out. I glanced at the phone before I spoke and it was after two in the morning.

93

"Who is this?" I sat up in the bed.

"Akeena, you insult me by asking." It had to be MJ.

"WHAT?" I yelled out and stood up. Armond never flinched and was still snoring.

"Bitch, you think you're running shit but I'd watch the company I keep. You may have gotten away with the few accidents you caused but trust me, when I say, I'm coming for you."

"You can try but.-"

"Oh you think because you got reconstruction of your face, I won't know who you are." He laughed loud in the phone.

"You have no idea what I look like."

"How does the saying go, keep your friends close and your enemies closer." He hung up without allowing me to respond.

How the hell did he know I had my face changed? It happened as soon as I got out the whorehouse. Fuck! Who in the hell was helping him? I needed to make some changes and fast. I ran down the steps and looked out all my windows only to see it pitch dark outside. I made sure all the doors and

windows were locked and walked in my home office. I've been

so careful in everything I planned. I had to find out who was

running their mouth and fast.

MJ

I had to laugh at the stupid bitch Akeena. Yea, she assumed no one knew who she was but I am fully aware. You see her son Baako, is in a gang over in Africa and they all work for me. He told me how she came looking for him and he had guns placed in her face. Little did she know, none other than Akeem's grandmother, who hated Akeem's father, wife and other kids; including Akeena, raised the son she had. The only reason she took Baako in, is because she felt bad.

Baako is the leader of the deadliest gang and drug game in Africa. He came over not too long ago for a meeting I had and pulled me to the side. He informed me of her looking for him and how he began watching her to see if she really wanted to get to know him. He found out she began looking for men to recruit for a takedown and assumed it was against his crew, so he sent someone in to pretend to be down for the cause. That's when he found out it was us she wanted.

He told me right away and the plans she had. Unfortunately, for her I destroyed all of them. She was able to pull the attack off with Joy because of my mom's recklessness and the only reason she hit Gabby, is because of PJ. Oh, I know all about Polo's other son being in cahoots with her. It was going to be fun making her suffer.

Armond seems to be the only one she feels something for. However, I had no idea what him or Akeena looked like. She was calling a meeting soon and I told the guy to snap photos. I may be the shit, but when you don't know who you're looking for it makes it harder.

That's why this shit with my kids and Morgan had to be fixed soon. My focus is separated between the two but I wanted my home life to be good. I didn't mean to snap on Morgan but at that moment it wasn't the time for her to be in her feelings.

Ok, we all know I messed up with Elaina but when she decided to take me back, the slate should've been wiped clean.

I'm not saying she had to be over it just like that but she damn sure don't need to make accusations.

When Logan came in pointing the gun at me with Camila in my arms, all I could think about was killing her. Yes, I had some feelings for her in the past but Morgan took them all and now no one could get close enough for me to even think about caring a little bit. I was happy my brother came with me to abuela's house; otherwise the situation could have turned out worse.

For those wondering why I didn't have security, that's easy. No one knew about my abuela's house except family and Logan. The reason she knew is because regardless of me not showing her off, she's been here a few times. My entire family knew I cared about her at some point. It never dawned on me that she'd follow me and make an attempt on me and my daughters' life.

This is the second time someone has gotten too close to me and the crazy part is, is that, it's women. I laugh thinking about it now. None of my enemies can get a few feet next to me and yet, the two bitches I fucked, did. They both wanted babies by me and one actually got one, while the other was mad I had any. Oh don't get it twisted, it's not as if they were a threat in my eyes but I guess you can never know.

****

Tonight, Alex and I were going out to have a few drinks and unwind. The club was aware we'd be there and made arrangements for our arrival. There would be a section closed off and security had spots to occupy. We were always cautious when we went out. Motherfuckers stayed lurking so it made sense to be the way we were.

My sister had both of my daughters at the house, which I thought would be too much but they were sleep when I left. When I first got shot and Morgan left, my grandmother on my mom side stayed with me. I appreciated the hell out of her because I had no strength the first few days.

Each day I grew stronger and so did the bond between, Camila and I. She cried a lot in the beginning, most likely from missing her bitch ass mother but each day it got better. Le Le wasn't too fond of sharing me and often smacked Camila in the face. I did laugh at first but Le Le thought it was funny too and kept doing it. I can see now that she was going to be bad as fuck.

"You good bro?" Alex asked getting in the car. It's been a couple of weeks since the shooting and he was still worried about me.

"Yea."

"You talk to Morgan yet?"

"Nah. She calls grandma and face times her to see Le Le. I told her not to let Morgan see Camila yet." Things weren't right between us and seeing my other daughter may distract her from coming home.

"You have to tell her."

"I will as soon as she brings her spoiled ass back." We both laughed.

I'm well aware of everything Morgan is doing in the states. I also know her ass hopped a flight over here today and is staying at a hotel. I had security on her but she didn't know and that's how it's going to stay. She was already able to elude two previously and I didn't need her trying it again. We parked in the back of the club and stepped in through the side door.

"Can I get you anything else to drink?" The waitress asked when we sat in the VIP area. This spot was closed off and had minimal light. The owner had an area in the corner that people could only see if they walked up on you. It was perfect for us to stay incognito.

We ordered a few rounds of drinks and a few hours later, we were both tipsy. Not enough to get caught slipping though. It felt good to sit back and enjoy myself without worrying. The enemies are still there, but until they step out the shadows, I'm good.

"Hey boss. This chick says she knows you." Sergio said.
I waved the woman back, knowing he patted her down first.
She had an attitude over it but in order to be next to me; you
have to do what you have to.

"What can I do for you miss?" I sipped on the Henny
left in my glass. She asked my brother to excuse himself. Alex
shook his head walking off and whispered something in the
guys' ear. It was probably to tell him not to let anyone in.
Sergio walked off with Alex.

"You can't help me at all but I think I can help you." I
glanced over her tight dress; strap up heels and licked my lips.
Shorty was thick as hell and my dick was brick hard.

"How are you going to do that?" She began unbuckling
my jeans, pulled my man out and slid down. I wasn't worried
about anyone seeing us because like I said, it's dark as hell.

"Fuck Morgan." I bit into her neck and grabbed her
face.

"Sssssss go slow baby." She moaned out and I guided her hips.

"Nah, you deserve this beating I'm about to put on you." I lifted her up, backed her against the wall and gave her exactly what she came for.

"I'm sorry Miguel. Oh Goddddd." She cried out scratching my back. I couldn't feel it too bad because of my shirt but it still hurt, nonetheless.

"What are you sorry about?" I now had her bent over the table.

"For accusing you and not listening. Baby, my legs are weak and I.-" she came again and I felt her cream running down my leg.

"What else." I grabbed her hair and lifted her up towards me.

"For leaving." She hopped off and turned around to face me.

"I swear it won't happen again. I love you so much Miguel and.-" she started crying. I wiped her tears and sat her on the table with her legs gapped open and slid back in. This time I was gentle.

"I love you too Morgan. When are you giving me my son?" I pumped a few more times and came inside, hoping I got her pregnant. I pulled my jeans up, grabbed some napkins off the table and wiped her down.

"I'm already pregnant." She covered her face and started crying again.

"What you mad?" She shook her head no.

"I wanted you to be there when I found out. Baby, I'm two months and it's been hell living without you and Le Le."

"You know where home is and you could've come anytime." She wrapped her arms around my neck.

"I know. Can I come home?" I ran my hand over my head.

"Miguel are you seeing someone else and before you snap, I'm asking you." I had a smile on my face. She remembered how I reacted.

"Never. You're still going to be my wife and make that the last time you ask. Its some things going on we need to discuss before you can come home." I stood her up.

"Is everything ok? What's wrong?" She ran her hand down my face. I swear I missed everything about her.

"Yea. Let's get out of here." I checked her over to make sure she didn't have anything leaking down her legs. Security moved out the way and had a big ass grin on his face as Morgan walked by.

"*PHEW*!" His ass dropped when the bullet pierced the back of his head. No one seemed to be paying attention and that was a good thing. I sent a message on my phone for someone to get here to clean the mess up.

"Baby."

"He saw me fucking you and I'll be damned if he lives to tell a soul."

"How do you know?"

"The look on his face. Morgan no one and I mean, no one, will ever be able to say they saw your pussy but me. I'm not sure when he began watching or how much he saw but the fact he did, cost him his life."

"But isn't he your security?"

"Nah. My security would never cross that line. Sergio is with Alex and mine is in the car. I really only came to relax and didn't want all them around. He was one of the club's employees." We went over to where Alex was at the bar with some chick.

"Time to go." Alex nodded and followed behind us.

"Sooooo, I guess y'all back together."

"We were never separated." Morgan said and smiled.

"Yea ok. Anyway I'm staying at the house with y'all. I promised my nieces I'd see them tomorrow."

"Nieces? I know Joy didn't have the baby yet and didn't tell me." I gave Alex a mean ass look through the rear view mirror. He shrugged his shoulders and chuckled.

"Morgan."

"Hell no nigga. Tell her when I'm out the car so when she beat your ass I don't have to witness it. I'm tired as fuck."

"I see you got jokes punk. Wait until I see Gabby. Oh, it's on."

"Whatever." We drove the rest of the way in silence. I could tell she had a lot on her mind after what my brother said but she waited to speak on it. When we got to the house Alex rushed out the car and ran in the house laughing. Morgan and I stepped out and I stood her in front of me as I leaned on the car.

"Morgan you know you and Le Le are everything to me." Her eyes were getting glassy as she shook her head.

"The shit with Carlotta is over but the possibility of having another daughter has always been there." She nodded. I lifted her chin to look at me.

"The baby is mine." She covered her mouth and began to cry harder. I held her until she calmed down.

"I'm sorry Miguel. I never thought you would have an outside child. How do we explain it to Le Le?"

"Le Le has been very mean to Camila." Morgan smirked when I said the name. I guess that's when it dawned on her, who I woke up asking for.

"As far as having an outside child. Morgan they are fraternal twins and you are her mother." She gasped.

"I know I should've asked you and I'm sorry, but baby if you're going to be with me, this is what it is. Wife or not, on paper you birthed her."

"I want to see her."

"Are you sure? I know it's a lot right now."

"I think I have the right to see my twin daughters, don't you?" We walked in and she of course checked on Le Le first and gave her tons of kisses.

Mariana yelled at her because she said Le Le gave her a hard time. I led her to the room with my grandmother and crazy as it sounds, Camila's ass was awake. My grandmother sucked her teeth and handed her off to Morgan.

"It's about time. This child refused to go to sleep. Close my door. I'm too old to be up this damn late." Morgan walked out with Camila and took her in our room.

"Miguel she looks just like Le Le. I mean they could be twins but with her bitch ass mother, her looks may change so keep them fraternal." Camila laid on her chest and literally two minutes later, she was knocked out. After we laid her in the crib, I took Morgan in the room and we both got in the shower.

"What are we going to do with three kids?" She asked washing me up.

"It doesn't matter as long as we're together."

"Yup."

"Well look into hiring a nanny this week."

"Ugh why? I can stay home with them."

"Not when you're going to be running your own business."

"Miguel no. I'm not ready and I wanted to do it on my own."

"Too late baby. You're my wife and if I want you to have something, I'm getting it. Of course, when the kids get older they'll be at one of my moms daycares."

"Damnnnnn mami, I missed you." I moaned out when she kneeled down and took me on her mouth. After she finished, I made love to my future wife as much as she could take. Ain't no way in hell, she's ever leaving me.

CJ

"Hey Connie." I heard once my mom finished feeding me. Everyday I swear, it felt as if I were a damn kid.

"Hey MJ. How are you?" It's been seven months and my cousin has finally decided to grace me with his presence.

"This is my wife Morgan. Well we aren't married yet, but you now what I mean." I heard them in the other room conversing for a while. After my mom finished feeding me and making sure I was presentable; she told MJ he could come in. Morgan came in too, looking as beautiful as ever. I wasn't checking my cousin's woman out but the fact remains, that she is beautiful.

"Hey CJ. How are you?" Morgan spoke and walked over to kiss my cheek.

"I'm alive." MJ sucked his teeth.

"Look. Its been quite some time now and I've asked MJ to come by for a reason." My mom said stepping inside the room. She asked Connie to run to the store and once she heard her pull off, the conversation started.

"I'm sorry MJ. I know it sounds like kid shit but I wanted my mother to love me. Yes, CiCi is my real mother but I was with my birth mother up until I was six years old. I'm not saying I shouldn't have known better because it would be a cop out. However, I do know it was stupid to even attempt to go against you." MJ had his head in the phone. Morgan was sitting on his lap and whispered something in his ear that made him pay attention.

"The only reason I'm here is because of these two." He pointed to my mom and Morgan. I nodded the best I could. He stood up and came towards me with an evil look. He had a gun at my temple and kept it there.

"Baby, calm down." Morgan stood in front of him.

"MJ, I think he learned his lesson. If you don't want to reverse the paralysis don't, but look at your cousin." She pointed to my mom who had a few tears coming down her face.

"Regardless of what went down, CiCi still loves you and I refused to see her cry." He walked over to my mom and hugged her.

"What do you want CiCi? Its up to you." I could see Morgan squeezing his hand. My mom walked over to me.

"CJ, I'm about to ask MJ to give you your life back. It means you will walk again and be allowed to resume activities to the best of your ability. But make no mistake." She squeezed my cheeks and made me face her.

"I am your mother and if you ever in your life put your hands on me again or come for our family in any way, shape of form; MJ won't be the one you have to worry about. I can promise, that I will fucking kill you with my bare hands."

"Ma." I've never heard her speak with so much venom in her voice.

"CJ, I don't think you understand. Your dad was willing to let you face the consequence MJ gave you, but I couldn't see it. However, you had me CJ. Me, of all people, out here begging for your cousin to keep you alive. I don't beg for anything so you better appreciate this second chance because I won't be there to rescue you again." She let my face go and walked out the room. MJ went out behind her and Morgan stood there staring at me.

I could see the disgust on her face but she didn't say anything at first. I've known her for years through my sister Patience and we were pretty cool. They did everything together and when her and MJ had that puppy love, she would tell me all the time, she'd marry him. I guess her dream is about to come true because MJ is head over heels in love with her.

"How could you go against your family CJ?" She was standing on the side of me.

"I thought my mother had my best interest at heart but as we all see, it was to benefit her." She nodded her head.

"You did all that for her and your real mother still had your back. CJ, your cousin could have killed you."

"I know Morgan."

"Please tell me you learned your lesson. I would hate for you to try him again and I have to kill you."

"Damn, maybe its best for everyone that I did die."

"Don't do that CJ."

"Don't do what?"

"Don't make it seem like what you did will be forgotten right away. You have to earn the right for everyone to respect you again." MJ and my mom came back in the room.

"Lets go baby." She grabbed MJ's hand and headed to the door.

"CiCi, you have what you need. Its now up to you. Oh and CJ, whenever you're better; remember from here on out, your every move will be watched." I didn't say anything and waited for them to leave. My mom came over to me and ripped me a new asshole again.

"You better appreciate what your mother is about to do." My father stood in the doorway with his face turned up and then walked away. I guess he was still in his feelings.

"CJ, make sure you thank MJ because.-"

"Hold up right there, Mrs. Thomas." We both stared in the direction of Connie's voice. She closed the door behind her and pointed a gun at my mother.

"What the fuck is going on?" I asked.

"I can't allow her to give you that."

"What? Connie what's really going on?" she asked my mom for the syringe, in which she handed it over.

"Tara hired me to make sure you never walk again. You see she's my best friend and once she heard I was taking care of you, she paid me a lot of money to make sure you never moved." She had a grin on her face.

"I thought you were in love with me."

"I do care about you but PJ is my man and we have two kids together. Matter of fact, he should be here in about..." She had her index finger on her chin.

"What you mean he should be here? Why would he come to my house?" My mom was pissed and I saw it all over her face.

"Oh. I told him MJ was here but I guess he didn't get her fast enough. It's ok though, because anyone related to him, PJ wants dead." I heard the doorbell ring and not even thirty seconds later, you could hear gunfire. My mom yanked my body off the bed and I hit the floor. I didn't feel it and my mom made sure she caught my head before it hit the ground.

"Where the fuck is my wife and son?" I heard my dad yelling.

"Right here baby. Is everything good?" My mom was now standing up and moved over to my dad. I heard a loud smack and then some sounds on the ground. I turned my neck and watching from under the bed, my mom was beating the hell out of Connie as my dad stood there watching.

"I want a new house." My mom stormed out the room and I heard another shot. Connie was dead and I could see the blood pouring out. My body was being lifted off the ground by my dad. He took me out the room and placed me in the wheelchair.

"CJ, I swear you better do right." He said as my mom came close with the syringe.

"You can have a bodyguard with me everyday and I still won't ever do anything remotely close as coming for my cousin." He nodded.

"This may hurt but soon you'll be able to move." She stuck it in my neck and at first we all sat there waiting to see.

"Ma, I think its working." I began wiggling my fingers.

It took a few hours for me to feel my entire body but a nigga

was happy as hell.

PJ

"Dammit. How the hell did they know we were coming?" I paced back and forth in my mothers house.

The plan was to go murk CJ, who we found out, was alive and well. The last Tara heard from him, they had slept together and he promised her, he'd come back. When he didn't, she figured MJ got to him and well; it's not much you can do when he does.

My sister had my niece who she named Cora Jane so she could have the initials like her dad. The name was ridiculous but we understood because like her, everyone assumed he was dead.

Fortunately for us, my girl was working as a LPN and in nursing school to become a RN. She knew someone, who knew someone that got her a good paying job. Unbeknownst to us, it landed her in CJ's house. She informed us how handicapped he was and instead of my sister feeling bad, she was pissed. I guess she felt he could've called her or something. He didn't or haven't even considered asking about the baby, from what we were told.

In the beginning, my girl hated going to work with him. She called him all kinds of names and said he deserved to be handicapped. We tried to get her to bring him outside but he refused and his parents wouldn't hear of it. He was embarrassed, while his parents, trusted no one.

However, in the last few months she spent more time with him then she did with me. I didn't think anything of it because he couldn't move. That was until she came home with a bracelet, clothes and other things for graduating. I asked her who gave her them to her and she told me him.

Now I'm not a stupid nigga and in order for him to give her all those things, she had to have been feeling him and vice versa. She kept telling me it wasn't like that so when she told me MJ was there; I wanted to see if she'd go through with the plan.

We pulled up at the house and it didn't seem like anyone was home. I had one of the guys open the door and he was hit in the middle of his chest by a bullet. CJ's pops continued letting off shots, which made all of us scatter. He was a beast with his shooting game too because we had to leave three dead motherfuckers on his lawn and drop two off at the hospital. I only came with that amount of people because I assumed MJ was there and could get at both of them.

"What happened?" Tara asked coming down the steps with my niece and nephew. Jacob was walking now and Cora was a few months old.

"We got to the house and his pops started shooting."

"Oh my God. Where's Connie?"

"I don't know. I've been calling her for over an hour. I'm hoping she didn't get hit. FUCK! I should've never allowed her to work there."

"PJ. I'm sure she's ok."

"If anything is wrong with her, I'm fucking you up."

"PJ, I.-"

"You nothing. I told you a long time ago to let his ass go but no, you wanted him to suffer. I told her to stop working for him months ago but again, you kept telling her to stay. I should've never listened to you."

"First of all PJ, Connie is grown. She could've said no anytime she wanted. You want to blame me, but all you had to do was whoop her ass and she would have never stayed."

"What you say?" I stood face to face with her.

"I know you put hands on her PJ. She told me and I didn't want to believe her until she showed me a video of you doing it. Connie recorded you beating the hell out if her. I told her to leave but she loved you too much and now look. You went there and instead of keeping her away, you let her go back. If you have anyone to blame, blame yourself." I punched her square in the face. My niece fell out her arms and my nephew started crying. I continued to beat on her until I became tired.

"PJ are you serious?" I heard one of my boys ask.

"Your niece is bleeding and your sister doesn't look like she's going to make it."

"Fuck her and them damn kids. I'm out." I snatched my keys off the table and passed my mother on the way in.

"What's wrong son?"

"What's wrong is you had kids by a bitch ass nigga whose blood runs through my veins. Therefore, so does his fucked up ways."

"What are you talking about? You are not him PJ."

"I'm not huh? You'll think differently when you lay eyes on your daughter." I chucked up the deuces, hopped in my car and pulled off.

I'm going to kill everyone out this motherfucker. I know people think I'm a punk and it's true but now that the one person I loved is probably gone, there's no need to waste any more time waiting on my brother and his bitch. For two years they claimed to have a plan in place and here we are still allowing these niggas to walk.

****

"What are you doing here?" My brother asked when I pulled up at their gate. After I beat my sisters' ass, I got on a plane to Africa. I had his address from a text message from him inviting me before but never came.

"Open the gate man. Got me out here yelling in a damn intercom." A few seconds later the gate split for me to enter.

I drove up and looked around at the scenery. They had a nice ass house, with a well-manicured lawn and trees all over. Shit, it looked like I was in Zamunda some damn where. *Where are the fucking elephants and tigers that walk freely?* I thought to myself. I parked my car, opened the door and

125

stepped out. My brother came towards me and I saw some woman, who I expect to be his chick standing at the door in just a robe. Now a nigga like me would smack the fuck out of my chick for coming to the door like that.

"What up bro? Its about time we finally met face to face." I smiled and nodded.

We met through Facebook like most people when he in boxed me, asking if we had the same dad. We messaged one another a few times and then exchanged phone numbers. We've spoken all the time since then. You may ask why didn't we face time one another, ain't no man doing that with another man, regardless if its his brother.

"This is my lady Akeena. Akeena, this is my brother PJ." She spoke and extended her hand. Now I'm a nigga before anything, so when she turned around, her ass sat up high enough for me to see under her robe and notice she had no panties on. She excused herself and went upstairs. Armond must've known then because he pushed me in front of him to go in a different direction.

"What brings you here?" I explained to him everything that went down and he agreed that it was taking too long. He also mentioned she was the one who had all the information and was very particular about giving him any of it. I asked why he thought it was and he shrugged his shoulders.

"I think you should go ahead with your plan, as far as Zariah goes and we can go from there. I mean its been two years already. What exactly is she waiting for?" Before he was able to answer she came in the room fully dressed.

"PJ, would you like to go out with us tonight? I'm sure one of the women from the strip club can show you a good time while you're here."

"Shit, you ain't said nothing but a word. I don't mind trying African pussy at all." They both laughed but a nigga was dead ass serious.

Aiden

"Why you on that petty shit?" I asked Shayla.

I was visiting my son and received a text from Joy. It was a photo of me laid back on the couch with my eyes closed, holding him. It was nothing but of course Shayla sent her the photo and put some bullshit ass text underneath about me staying the night.

"I don't know what you're talking about."

"I bet you will if I choke the shit out of you." Her eyes got big as hell.

"AJ, I don't understand why we can't be together. I have your first son and I was here before her." I laid my son in the bassinet she had in the living room. I pulled my sagging jeans up and walked in the kitchen to where she went.

"Shayla, you were someone I was fucking, nothing more. I thought we could be together but it didn't work out."

"It's because she interfered."

"How did she interfere when she doesn't even live here? Listen to yourself Shayla. You're blaming a woman for something she was unaware of. I hadn't slept with you those last two weeks before my accident and told you, I wouldn't be with you."

"AJ, I just want.-" She grabbed on my dick and began rubbing it. I had to chuckle at her stupid ass.

"You want what Shayla?" She bit down on her lip and I grabbed her hand.

"You want this dick so you can run back and throw it in her face. Guess what?"

"Stop AJ. You're hurting me."

"You'll never feel this dick again for two reasons. One... because you are a fucked up individual. And two... Joy is mad with me now but she's the only one who will ever have it again. I suggest you move the fuck on." I pushed her out my way.

"You know for someone to be older than me, you're surely acting like a damn teenager. My son may have you as a mother now, but make no mistake; he won't miss you when I take him."

"AJ you would take my son." I couldn't even tell if she was upset. Her reaction remained flat and if I didn't know any better; I bet she assumed her having my kid would keep me or make me sleep with her.

"Don't give me a reason to." I went back in the living room and kissed my son on the cheek. I had to leave before I beat the hell out of her and I'm no woman beater. Sometimes women knew which buttons to push to make a man lay hands on her and that's exactly what it felt like she was trying to do.

I jumped in my car and dialed Joy's number. She hasn't answered any of my calls since she left a few weeks ago. I missed the hell out of her and decided to catch a flight over there. I called Alex and asked him to meet me at the airport in a few hours and not to mention my arrival. I didn't get there until after eleven at night, their time. He took me straight to the estate and opened the door for me and left. He told me he didn't want any parts in her yelling at me.

This was my first time in her place and the shit was nice as hell. She had glass windows in the entire house; even the staircase was made of glass. She had a white living room that was purely for show and a regular living room. The dining room looked just as expensive.

I continued giving myself a tour and realized she didn't need me at all; living like this. I knew they had money and I've been on the estate before but damn each house was different. Her house made mine look like the projects. Don't get me wrong, I have money but they are definitely beyond wealthy. Shit, I don't know what category they fall under.

I took my shoes off and walked up the steps. It was so many damn doors; I had to open each one. Every room was big with different colors. I got to the last door and opened it, only to have a gun pointed in my face. I had to laugh because she must've known it was me. No one else can get on this estate.

"Get that shit out my face." I moved past her as I removed my clothes. I walked straight in the bathroom and started the shower. I only knew it was one in here because the light was on.

"What are you going here AJ? Shouldn't you be somewhere entertaining your baby mother?" I heard sarcasm in her voice as she yelled from the other room. I continued ignoring her and washed up. I shut the water off when I finished and stepped out. I walked in the room butt ass naked and found her lying in the bed. I didn't say anything to her and pulled the covers back.

"Stop AJ."

"Nah. You got all that mouth so I'm about to give you what you want."

"I don't want shit from you." I grabbed her ankles and pulled her to the edge of the bed.

"Go homeeeeee. Oh fuckkkkkk!" She moaned out when my tongue slid up and down her bottom lips. I felt her hips moving as she grinded on my face. I put two fingers inside and her body began to shake. Her hand went on the top of my head.

"Yes AJ. Yessssssss." Her nectar shot out on my face and chin. I decided to give her another one and watched her shake again and yell my name. I stood up and stared down at her as my dick touched her clit.

"Can I have some of my pussy?" She nodded her head yes and opened up wider.

"Damnnnnnn Joy. I missed you." I wasn't in her longer than five minutes and came. We both laughed.

She sat up and took me in her mouth to get me hard again. I had to grip the sheets to stifle the moan trying to escape. Joy's head game was the best I had. I lifted her up before I came and guided her down my rod.

She threw her head back and rode me so good my damn toes were curling. She turned around and rode me cowgirl style and I almost came right away. Watching her ass go up and down and the way her juices leaked out, had me rock hard. I sat up, gripped her breasts and kissed her back, as my hand found its way to her protruding nub.

"Squeeze that pussy and make your man cum at the same time." She did what I asked and we both released.

"Shit! I needed that." Joy lifted herself off me and went in the bathroom to clean herself up. I followed to so the same.

"I miss you baby." I kissed her neck and stared at her in the mirror. She turned around and her stomach pushed me away a little.

"Ok you came, you saw, we fucked, you can go home now."

"Shut that shit up. I ain't going no damn where." I entered her from behind and beat that pussy up again as we stared at each other in the mirror. I loved the hell out of Joy and she wasn't about to leave me that easy. We were lying in the bed after we finished sexing each other down and I decided to apologize.

"I'm sorry for jumping down your throat at the hospital and not telling you she had the baby. It wasn't intentional and she called me after the delivery. I only stayed to make sure she didn't ask the lady to change the results. It may have only been two hours and the results didn't come to the next day but I didn't trust her. Shit, since you been gone, I had him retested just to be sure."

"AJ."

"Nah, fuck that. She can play like she in love all she wants but I'm still going to be sure. I left her alone so there was no telling who she'd been with." I was serious as hell right now. Women are scandalous as hell and I'd hate to find out

eighteen years later the kid isn't mine.

"But you named him after you. I thought.-" I cut her off.

"She had already given him the name and signed the

birth certificate before I got there. Don't ask me how but I

never saw it and she wouldn't allow me to sign it. Evidently,

since I questioned the paternity they felt it didn't matter if I

signed it. Something was fishy about that whole thing but if

you want him to be named after me too, then do it."

"No, its ok. Maybe we're having a girl." I could see she

was upset but Shayla was sneaky and did everything so fast, I

didn't have time to correct shit. It was all to hurt Joy and she

did a good job at it but she still lost because I would never

choose her.

****

"What up?" I answered groggily into the phone. Its

been two days since I got to Puerto Rico and I was still here.

Joy was eight months now and I was scared to leave and she delivers without me. Yes, her and my sister were a week apart in their pregnancy.

"Yo, you need to look at your phone." DJ said and I told him I would call him back.

"Everything ok." Joy asked coming out the bathroom. I didn't even realize she was awake yet. We had been out shopping all day yesterday and had sex most of the night.

"Yea, hold on." I damn near dropped my phone when I opened up the message.

"I'm about to kill that bitch." I jumped up and threw my clothes on. I could see Joy tearing up with her hand covering her mouth as she watched the disturbing video I got.

"Is he ok?" She began putting clothes on too.

"I have no idea." Pass me my phone. I dialed DJ back.

"Where did this video come from?"

"Man, I don't know. Savannah said she posted it online and somehow sent the video out to mad people."

"Can you go over there and get my son please? I'm in Puerto Rico and its going to take me a minute to get there. I'm calling my parents too."

"I'm already on the way there. When Savannah showed me the video, I jumped in the car." We spoke for a few more minutes and I hung up to make another call.

"MJ, are you around. I need a favor."

"I'm home, what's up?" I explained what happened and asked if I could use the jet. Him and Morgan met us outside and all of us hopped in the car and sped to the airport.

The entire ride to the states all I could think of was the video. Shayla had my son on the couch lying there, smacking him in the face over and over because he wouldn't stop crying. My son is only a month old so my ass was fuming. The worse part was her tossing him in the bassinet and shaking the shit out of it. My son rolled back and forth, hitting his face on the sides.

My blood was boiling when we landed and MJ had to pull me to the side to get me calm. Joy wobbled behind me and I made sure to ask if she were ok. We hopped in the awaiting truck and MJ told him to speed to the address, which took another twenty minutes to get to. I jumped out before the driver even came to a complete stop and ran over to my mom. Shayla's mom was standing at the door with the cops not allowing anyone to go it. I'm glad they stayed until I got here.

"Well look who finally came to see their son."

"Bitch move." I tried to move past and the cop stood in front of her as if that meant anything.

"I'm sorry sir but the occupant doesn't want anyone to go inside."

"She has my son and posted some shit online where she's beating on him."

"Baby, DJ told him but they didn't want to see the video or let us in." My mom was standing there upset and so was my sister.

"Yo, let him the fuck in NOW!" MJ yelled out and when the cop noticed who he was, his eyes got big and he moved fast as hell. Her mom still stood there until I pushed her out the way.

I walked in the house and couldn't help but turn my nose up at the smell. It was dishes piled up in the sink and the garbage overflowed. I went in the living room and she wasn't in there. I looked in the bassinet and my son wasn't in there, which made me haul ass upstairs. What I saw next, almost gave me a heart attack.

Shayla

The day AJ left from seeing our son was the last straw for him treating me like shit. He and I were sex partners in the beginning, well; I was mostly giving him head at the beginning but once he put that dick in my life, that was it. I knew we were destined to be together. Unfortunately, the Joy bitch threw a monkey wrench in our happiness. AJ can say we weren't together all he wanted but he was at my house everyday until the two weeks he before he had the accident.

He did send me messages declaring us to be over but I didn't believe him. If he would've just come over and told me what was really wrong, I could've fixed the problem. I know his accident had him incapacitated for a while but I also knew he would want to have sex when he woke up.

See what no one knew was that AJ, had opened his eyes right before I hopped on top of him and closed them back. I guess the light was too bright. I saw my chance to get pregnant by him and took it. Yea, he was weak but he still came inside me, so it is what it is.

I didn't call him when I delivered because my mom was here and I know he would've told her how I really got pregnant and she didn't need to know. I got a kick out of Joy's face when I mentioned my son and even offered for them to come see him. I had no idea they would reveal to my mom what happened. Long story short, he came up to my room, they argued, she left and he ran after her. That shit pissed me off and I knew then, I had to work harder to keep him.

When he grabbed my wrist and almost broke it for touching his dick, I knew I needed to do something to grab his attention. I set my phone down on my coffee table and changed my son. I was going to record me baby talking to him and ask him to come home but then he started crying.

I don't know what happened after that but I started smacking my son in the face. It only made him scream louder and infuriate me more. I tossed him in the bassinet and tried rocking him but he kept kitting himself on the side of the bassinet.

I finally got him to be quiet and left him to get my phone. I stopped the video and looked at it. I was hysterical laughing at me smack him while he cried. It was funny the way his head went back and forth but even funnier as he swayed from side to side in the bassinet.

I posted it on FB thinking everyone would find it just as funny and then sent it to him. I began getting notifications from people asking who I was and where did I live. Some said they were sending the cops the video and that my child needed to be taken away. I never realized people could be so mean. I removed it from FB and prayed no one called the cops.

I got a text message from AJ saying he was on his way to get my son. Now at first, I thought he was coming to visit or take him out until his mom, sister, best friend and few others showed up, trying to get in. By that time my mom had come over and asked me what was going on and called the cops herself.

Not too long after the cops got there I heard AJ's voice and looked outside. I had a smile on my face because the video allowed me to see him again. The frown turned upside down when I saw the pregnant bitch of a girlfriend get out with him. I ran upstairs, opened the window and really gave everyone a show. He wanted to play with me; I was going to teach his dumb ass a lesson.

"Shayla, don't do this." AJ said as he walked in the room. I could hear people screaming outside as I held my son upside down out the window.

"Don't do what AJ? Huh?"

"Give me my son." He moved closer and I shook my hand to make little Aiden dangle some more. He began crying and I felt myself getting pissed again.

"Oh now he's your son."

"He's always been Shayla. Why are you doing this?"
He moved closer.

"Because you are supposed to be my man, not hers. We were together first and that bitch came and took you from me."

"Shayla, I swear, I'll leave her and come to you. Just bring my son in the window."

"Why would you want to be with me now?"

"Shayla what are you doing? Bring that baby in the window." My mom yelled and I had to laugh at her. My mother is a piece of work and should be happy my son is hanging out the window and not her. I hated her for not helping me get AJ back. All she kept saying was *move on honey if he doesn't want to be with you.* How do you move on without the person you love?

"I'm going to count to three Shayla and if you don't bring him in, I'm going to knock you the fuck out."

"Oh you'll hit me over this fucking baby. I knew you were a woman beater."

"Shayla please bring the baby in." My mom now had tears in her eyes.

"One…" AJ said and I sucked my teeth.

"You love him more than me AJ."

"Two…" He started moving closer.

"If you hit me, the baby falls so either way you're losing."

"Three…" I smirked and let go. He ran over to me and looked out the window. I stood there with my arms folded.

He turned around and it was like the devil showed up. His fist connected with my face and I literally fell back against the wall. I tried to block the constant blows he rained on my face but it was no use. His feet were connecting to my body as well. I think I blacked out for a second but when I woke up he was still hitting me. By the time people got him off me, blood

was everywhere and I couldn't move.

"You should've killed yourself." He said and I heard a

gun go off.

Joy

That bitch was crazy as hell. Who in the hell beats on a baby like that and then dangles him out the window because a man doesn't want her? When we saw the baby hanging out, my heart dropped and I had to sit in the truck. MJ wouldn't allow me or Gabby to stand out there. At this moment, either of us could deliver at any time and MJ said it was best if we stayed in the truck. Morgan hopped in the front and locked the doors.

"If she drops the baby, AJ is going to kill her." I said and they both agreed. More cops started to arrive, as well as an EMT, Paramedic and fire truck. She was so busy fussing that she never realized the firemen had the ladder almost at the window.

"Please let them get the baby in time." Gabby said and started crying. Morgan and I told her it was going to be ok.

"Noooooo." We heard AJ's mom yell and looked back at the house.

The ladder was a few inches away from the window but Shayla was still able to drop him. Luckily all the men were at the bottom of the window and caught her. They handed him to AJ's mom and she jumped in the back of the ambulance with them.

She told MJ and DJ to go get her son because he most likely was upstairs killing her. That made me get out the car and go inside. Sure enough, my man was beating the shit out of her. The cops came running up and MJ dared any of them to stop him.

"MJ, please make him stop. He needs to go check on his son." I told him and they finally got him off her.

"Are you ok?" He asked. Once I told him yes he went back over to Shayla, said a few words and shot her twice in the head. No one said a word. He grabbed my hand and had me follow him.

"I want him arrested for killing my daughter." Her mom said on the way down the steps. I let go off AJ's hand and he tried to keep me from going to her but I had to.

"I wish you would get him arrested."

"He killed.-"

"So what. Your daughter tried to kill his son. You saw her crazy ass holding him out the window and that's after she posted a video of her beating on him. She's lucky he killed her. Had it been me, I would've made her suffer a hundred times more for what she did. I suggest you go plan her funeral and stay the fuck out my man's face and life."

"How dare you?"

"Easy. That's my man and stepson and no bitch or man will ever threaten him or his father. You may not know me and be happy you don't because I can guarantee, you don't want none of this."

"You good sis." I heard Morgan say.

"Yea. I just had to get this bitch in check. Talking about she wants AJ arrested."

"And he will be. You bitches think.-" Is all she got out before I punched her in the face. She stumbled back and I hit her again until AJ grabbed me off. It didn't matter because Morgan followed up and started hitting her. Of course, MJ had a fit and pulled her off. The woman had blood everywhere but it was her fault.

"You know I'm fucking you up later." AJ said grinning and helping me in the truck.

"Whatever."

"That ass whooping could've waited until you had my baby." MJ was cursing Morgan out in the front seat too. I looked at my phone and it was a message from her.

Morgan: *I don't know why your brother acting like he mad. I'm going to fuck his brains out later and he'll forget this even happened.*

151

Me: Same here. I sent a smiley face emoji. MJ snatched the phone out Morgan's hand as we stepped in the hospital.

"Oh yea Morgan. I bet you don't feel this dick for a while now." He put her phone in his pocket. The two of us busted out laughing. We waited for AJ to find out where his mom and son were and walked behind him to the room.

"Is he ok?" AJ asked. They had little Aiden in a crib with an IV on his arm, attached to a splint.

"They're waiting for blood work to come back. The CAT scan was clear of his head but they want to do a MRI too. Did you know he had pneumonia?"

"WHAT?"

"Yea. The doctor said his fever was very high and he had fluid on his lungs." The more his mom spoke, the angrier he got.

I picked little Aiden up and sat down. He was only a month old and had gone through enough for a lifetime because his momma couldn't take rejection. He started crying and AJ's mom handed me a bottle. I was about to feed him when an excruciating pain went through my back.

"AJ, take him. Oh my God." He rushed over to me and lifted him out my arms.

"What's wrong?" He looked scared as hell.

"I don't know. Fuckkkk!" MJ started laughing.

"Your ass in labor sis." Morgan and AJ's mom jumped up.

"Joy, can I please come in the room? I missed little Aiden being born and.-"

"You don't have to ask me that. Of course you can. AJJJJJJJJJ!" I screamed and he ran out the room. A nurse came back with a wheelchair.

"MJ, can you?-" AJ was going to ask him to stay in the room but MJ beat him to it.

"Go ahead. I won't let anything happen to him. Good luck sis and I hope my niece or nephew gives you hell, since you and Morgan want to pop shit." I flipped him the bird and waited for the nurse to wheel me out. AJ called my dad and the entire family was on their way over here.

****

"She is gorgeous." My mom said holding my daughter Alexa Rose Rowan. She came ten hours and fifteen stitches later. She weighed almost nine pounds; therefore, I had to be cut in order for them to get her out. AJ thought the shit was beyond amazing. His ass said, *"A whole body came out your small ass pussy."* His mom smacked him on the back of his head. That's what his ass gets.

"She resembles little Aiden a lot." I told AJ and he smiled.

"What the hell are we going to do with two babies this close in age?"

"Don't worry baby. We'll get through it." I pulled him in for a kiss.

"Soon as you're healed, I'm fucking the shit out of you." He whispered in my ear, making me grin hard as hell.

AJ walked everyone out and I laid there staring at both of my kids. Yes, I claimed little Aiden as mine being his mom is no longer with us. The doctors allowed him to come in the room with me since they were keeping him overnight for observation anyway. He started to whine a little so I reached over in the crib that was directly next to me, picked him up and fed him. Alexa started to cry as soon as AJ stepped in the room. He lifted her up, changed and fed her.

"Thanks Joy."

"Why are you thanking me?" I had little Aiden on my shoulder to burp him.

"For taking in my son."

"Our son will be fine and you should've known I wouldn't turn my back on him or you." He sat on the side of me and pulled something out his pocket.

"Will you marry me?" I nodded my head crying as he slipped the ring on.

"I had an entire speech planned out but at this moment, all I want to hear is yes."

"I would have been fine with you just putting the ring on my finger."

"I had to say something." He leaned in to kiss me with a grin on his face. I guess he wasn't lying when he claimed he would be my first and last.

****

"Do you think he'll look for his mom when he gets older?" I asked AJ as I put clothes on little Aiden.

We were taking Alexa to her first doctors' appointment.

Afterwards we were meeting with my brother Alex for dinner,

who hadn't been over to see her yet. Him and MJ were plotting

on something big. From what AJ told me, they know where the

people are that caused me and Gabby's accident and were

waiting to attack. I wish they would hurry up and get it over

with but then again my brother doesn't operate like that. When

he does hit, I'm sure it will be big.

"If he does we can tell him the truth or let him think

you're his mom. Shit, look at Morgan and your brother's

situation." I thought about what he said and he's right; little

Aiden didn't need to know his mother was certified crazy.

"I'll ask MJ to fix it so the birth certificate will say it."

He had a smirk on his face.

"AJ. I know damn well you didn't do it already." He

shrugged his shoulders and walked out with Alexa. I put Aiden

on my shoulder and followed him in my daughters' room.

"Aiden Rowan!" I shouted and he turned around.

"Look. MJ said it was the best thing and for us to get it done. He didn't want anyone questioning his paternity and since he was in town, I figured we get it done. Are you mad?" I laid Aiden in the crib.

"I'm not mad but if we're going to be married, we have to communicate. Don't assume you know what I'm going to say and jump into a situation without me. As you can see, I will have your back regardless. I'll never contradict anything you say or do, well in public anyway."

"You better not." I smacked him on the arm.

"I'm sorry baby and it won't happen again." I left the room and went into ours to shower and get ready.

Now that I'm staying in the states with him, we both decided to have a house built from the ground up. Of course, I'll have full control of it. He knows if I'm going to be here, I have to be comfortable. Plus after I told my dad he proposed, he decided to foot the bill, so a bitch is going all out. AJ wasn't happy about my dad paying for it because he had money too but my dad explained to him that it was a wedding present.

Aiden is like his dad when it comes to handouts. He feels if someone offers or gives him something, it will come with a cost. In this case, the cost is me and our kids. I know men have a certain image to maintain but my parents have always given us the best and they're not about to let us settle. He may be the son of a BOSS, but I'm the daughter of a SAVAGE BOSS and in the end, what he says goes.

"I got it baby." I told AJ when the doorbell rang. I had just brought Alexa down while he was getting dressed, placed her in the car seat and Aiden was in my arms.

"Hello Joy." She said and I slammed the door in her face. I wasn't trying to be rude. I had to put my son down in case things got hectic. I put both of the babies in the living room, which is away from the door and went back to open it.

"That was rude." She said with a smirk on her face.

"And so are you showing up uninvited." I had my arms folded. I stared at Shayla's mom and waited for her to speak.

"Can I come in?"

"Not at all. Whatever you need to say can be said right here."

"I understand." I stood there waiting. It seemed as if she were scared to speak.

"I'm sorry about everything that went down with my daughter and I would like to know if its possible to get to know my grandson?" This is what I was afraid of. How can she spend time with her grandson and he not question his paternity later? However, I'm going to be the bigger woman and allow it. AJ may not be as accepting as me though.

"We're about to go to the doctors but if you want, I'll let you see him for a few minutes." I offered for her to enter the house and showed her Aiden. She instantly started to cry.

"He looks just like Shayla." Now I wanted to smack her. Aiden resembled his father and sister. I know it's a possibility he could have his mom looks eventually but right now, he doesn't. I see now, her pettiness is going to make me fuck her up.

"I'll be right back." I picked Alexa up and gave her some alone time with him.

"Who was at the door?" I sat on the bed and stared at how good my fiancé looked. I put Alexa in the bed, put pillows around her and my arms around his waist.

"Shayla's mom stopped by and.-" He took off down the stairs. I ran behind him when I heard my son screaming and was flabbergasted at the shit I saw.

"Please let me go." AJ had her up by the throat.

I didn't know what happened until I walked over and saw blood on my son. I picked him up and she had a small knife in his side. I called 911 immediately and told AJ not to kill her. The cops locked her up and that's because we had to let them know what happened so child protective services didn't take him. I made a call to MJ and asked him to handle that and I wanted her shipped to Puerto Rico. I had something special planned for her. Her daughter got away but she won't.

"What happened to him?" AJ's mom was hysterical when she came in. We told her and she was pissed. His father came in and held his mom tight. I swear I didn't know whose relationship I envied more, theirs or my parents. The doctor came in a few minutes later, introduced himself and told us what was going on.

"Your son will be fine. The person who did this didn't go far enough but on a baby, any puncture of the skin is far. He has about ten stitches on his side, otherwise, he's good. He's asleep right now and probably will be for a while."

"Thank you so much. Can we see him?" I asked.

"Yes and who is this one here?" He looked at Alexa who was asleep.

"His sister."

"Wow! Are you sure they're not twins? Your son looks just like her." AJ smiled like a big ass kid.

"My DNA is the shit." I smacked his arm and followed the doctor. His dad shook his head laughing.

"Awww look at my baby." I started crying when I saw the bandages on his stomach.

I couldn't wait to return home and torture the fuck out of her. I already sent my cousin Ricky a text not to start without me. Once he heard what happened he wanted to pour acid on her. I had to beg him to wait. His ass told me I had to order him two Louis V purses online that hadn't come in the stores yet and a pair of red bottom boots. My cousin is a diva for real but I loved him.

We were sitting in the hospital room when my brother Alex walked in. He had the phone on his ear and I could tell from his conversation he was talking to MJ. I knew he was coming here to check on Gabby but not this early in the morning. He gave me a hug; AJ a man hug and picked Aiden up who was now wide awake. All Alex spoke about was when his kids came and how he would spoil them.

I hit Gabby up and asked where she was. Once I read the text, I told Alex and he was pissed. He put Aiden down and rushed out the hospital. I don't know what's going on with them but Gabby is playing a dangerous game with my brother. She better get it together quick.

CJ

"It's about time you woke up." She looked around and when her eyes landed on me, they grew big.

"What are you doing here? I thought you were dead." Tara said trying to sit up in the hospital bed.

"You knew I wasn't dead. That's why you sent your so called best friend over to keep an eye on me." I moved closer to her slowly. It's been three weeks since my cousin gave my mom the medicine to reverse the paralysis and I must say, a nigga is appreciative as hell. I had been doing physical therapy everyday and even though I'm not as strong as I used to be, being able to move around at all, is enough for me.

"Who told you?"

"She did, right before taking her last breath." Tara covered her mouth.

"The entire time I thought she would be the one for me. I mean, she let me eat her pussy plenty of times, she played with herself in front of me and almost got my dick hard."

"Connie wouldn't do that." I smiled and pushed the little bit of hair out her face.

"Bitches will do anything if they assume no one will find out."

"How could you kill her?"

"Why would you send her there? Tara, we may have only been fucking, but you were carrying my child. Once you found out I was alive, why didn't you come to me?"

"Fuck You CJ. You're not going to make me the bad guy."

"Fuck me. Really! I was paralyzed and couldn't move. I refused to leave the house and fell into depression. Had you come over, you would've saw for yourself. My daughter didn't even know me when I met her." She turned her head and wiped the tears.

I know Tara had feelings for me and I cared about her too but what she did is unforgivable. I was in a fucked up situation and instead of her being there for me she sent someone to watch and almost kill me.

"Why in the hell would you name her Cora Jane?"

"So she could have the same nickname as you." I had to laugh.

"That's the dumbest shit I ever heard and she's not a boy. Her looks and my blood running through her veins is enough to remind her of who she is."

"Have you seen her?" She asked me with a serious look on her face.

"I have. She's also been tested so I can be sure she's mine. And as of right now, she will be living with me."

"Don't take my baby CJ."

"You are out your rabid ass mind if you think for one minute my daughter will live in that filthy ass house any longer. Not only that, if your brother can whoop your ass, there's no telling what he'd do to her. It's bad enough he hooked off with her in your arms. Luckily, she fell on the couch and then rolled off. It only left a gash on her forehead but that's enough for me to take her." I only found that out because her mom told me when I called looking for Tara. She said PJ became enraged over what went down with Connie and took it out on his sister.

A few days after I got the feeling in my body, I asked my mom to take me to see the baby. My father refused to allow her to go over there and took me himself. I didn't get out the car so my dad went in and got the baby. Tara's mom came out and told us everything we needed to know and from then on, my daughter has been staying with us.

She cried a lot the first two days but after my sister Sienna and Patience came over, she was good. My mom began spoiling her like she did my nephew and that was it. You can barely put her down and if she cries, my mom picks her ass right back up.

"He was mad because of what happened to Connie." I couldn't believe she was defending him. Anything could've been wrong with our daughter and she still had his back. I heard how loyal she is to him but that's ridiculous.

"I don't care how pissed he was, his ass knows better. I guess it's true when they say the apple doesn't fall far from the tree. I heard y'all father was a true fuck nigga; well I guess it runs in the family. My daughter won't ever see anything like that again."

"CJ please. I need my kids."

"You only need them because of the money their fathers have and you aren't even using it for them." The door opened and in walked my father who had been taking me everywhere I needed to go. I asked him and my mom to stand outside while I spoke to her first.

Our father son relationship was finally getting back to where it used to be. I hate to say it but this shit opened my eyes to who's supposed to be in my life. I never should've let Denise's greedy ass get in my head but trust, no one from my past will ever get that again.

If you're wondering why I say that; well my aunt, who is Denise sister has been trying to get in touch with me through my father. I told him to let her think I was dead. I didn't need any negativity in my life and from what my mom tells me, her and Denise were in cahoots with one another, so I'm sure she'd try her hand at getting my parents too.

"You ready." He stood there, looked at Tara and shook his head.

"Say hi daddy." My mom came strolling in with Cora, whose name will be changed.

"Oh my God. Cora. Come to mommy." That's how dumb Tara is. My daughter is only a few months old and has no idea what that means. She was lying on my moms shoulder looking around.

"Tara, it's too bad you couldn't get your life together and tried coming for my son." She handed Cora to my dad.

"You will learn sooner or later that revenge will get you nowhere." My mom punched her in the face and kept hitting her. My dad handed me Cora and broke it up. Tara tried to hit back but my moms' hands were no joke. Cora had a smile on her face as she sat on my lap. I think she was happy to see her mother get beat up; I know I was.

"Goodbye." I stood up and walked out the room. I had Cora in my good arm and we all left the hospital together. That part of my life was over and it was time to move on.

Gabby

"One more week Miss Gabby. We want to keep the twins in as long as possible. Are you excited?" The doctor asked as I rubbed the gel off my stomach. She said the same shit every week.

"Yes I am. I-" the door flung open and there stood Alex. I hadn't seen him since my accident but I've been updating him as far as the twins go.

"Lay back down Gabby. The doctor is going to do another ultrasound."

"No. She just finished." He laughed shaking his head.

"You have it confused. It wasn't a question."

"Excuse me sir." My doctor appeared to be nervous, yet, stood there with her arms folded.

"You're excused. Turn the machine on and repeat the ultrasound."

"Alex don't come in here demanding things when you haven't been to one appointment."

"Doctor can you excuse us for a moment? Don't go far because the ultrasound will be repeated." I stood up and he pushed me down on the table but not hard. The door closed and he stared at me.

"Gabby, I don't give a fuck about the attitude you have. What I do care about, are my damn kids."

"Oh now you care?" He squeezed my cheeks together.

"Gabby, you take me for this punk ass guy that won't fuck you up. I have a side to me you don't want to see. As far as being here for appointments, stop going around telling people I'm a deadbeat father already. You haven't informed me of any of these appointments and when I call you don't answer. Now I gave you time to get over the bullshit lie your ex told you but this kiddie behavior is for teenagers."

"I'm not acting.-"

"Yes you are. Gabby you just turned twenty but you can't tell. If you want to know what happened with Julia you should've asked. Instead you believed your ex over the nigga you're with."

"But you left me here and didn't call."

"So what Gabby. My brother told you before, when I can tell you shit I will. I never cheated on you and my mom gave you the code to our estate. I had plans for us but I'll be damned if I'm going to raise three kids at a time. I got enough shit going on in my life then to be worried about these temper tantrums and silent treatments. Then you running around making motherfuckers think I don't want my kids. What the fuck is wrong with you?" I busted out crying. He stood there staring at me. I thought he would at least give me a hug or ask if I were ok but he stood there waiting for me to finish.

"Ok doc. You can come in." Alex said after opening the door.

"Is she ok? Miss Gabby, did.-"

"I wish you would ask if I hit her."

"But she's crying."

"So the fuck what. Isn't that what happens when women are pregnant? They cry at any and everything. Turn the machine on and do what you're supposed to."

"Mr.-"

"Don't worry about what my name is. Lay back Gabby." I did what he said and she performed another ultrasound. Alex asked what we were having and she told him one of each. He had a big ass smile on his face. I on the other hand already knew.

"Get dressed and go straight home."

"Sir, you don't have to speak to her that way." My doctor tried to defend me but when I saw the look in Alex eyes, I knew she messed up.

"Listen here doctor. That woman and the two kids in her stomach are my concern, not yours. What I do and how I speak to her is not your business, nor is it an invitation for you to add your two cents. You are a gynecologist, not a psychologist so unless you're changing professions, it's in your best interest to shut the fuck up."

"Sir, I was being nice and gave you another ultrasound and this is how you speak." He moved in closer.

"First off... I think you need to check her charts and see who's fronting the bill for this appointment and all the rest." The doctor didn't say a word.

"Then I'm going to need you to get all her files together because after today, she will no longer be a patient here. Last but not least; you showing me my kids was going to happen regardless. Just because she was being negligent and not informing me of these appointments doesn't mean shit. Had I known, I would've been here. And for the record, any man who gets a chick pregnant has the right to see his kids inside her womb just like the mother. Hell, we are the ones who placed the kid or kids in there." My doctors' mouth was on the floor.

"That's motherfuckers problems now. Not knowing what's going on but always running their mouth. Let's go Gabby and don't make me say it again." I stood up.

"Ummmm. Miss Rowan I apologize if I crossed the line. You have been coming here for years and.-"

"Don't worry about it. He's very protective of me and to be honest, it turned me on. I'm going to have to have a lot of sex to make up for his time loss." She turned beet red. The two of us talked about a lot but I'm sure that threw her for a loop.

"Alex." I yelled out as I wobbled my big ass out the room. I was eight months and everyone was shocked that I made it this far. They decided that in a week that it's best for me to be induced through C-section and I couldn't agree more. These babies were driving me crazy with the kicking.

I stepped out the doctors' office and saw him standing against a black truck. Alex has always been handsome but watching him boss up on me, made him even sexier. I made my way to him and noticed him lick his lips as he stared at my breasts. They were pretty big and on display in my V-neck t-shirt. He pulled me in front of him and kissed my cheek. *What the fuck?* Why in the hell is he kissing my cheek? He continued his conversation on the phone in Spanish. And I swear, I came on myself. If you ever get the chance to be with someone who speaks another language, you'll understand why it turns me on.

"You good ma." He disconnected the call and held my hand as he walked me to my car.

"Yea."

"After today, I don't want you driving. Matter of fact, Mark come here." One of his security guards came to where we were.

"Drive her home and I'll meet you there."

"Why can't you drive me?" I was now pouting.

"If you wanted me to drive you, this appointment would've never been a secret." I rolled my eyes.

"Oh you thought because I hugged you and kissed your cheek, we're good?"

"Ugh yea."

"Nah. You're still on my shit list. I missed everything with this pregnancy. Today is the first time I was able to see my kids."

"Alex.-"

"I don't want to hear it. You knew exactly what you were doing. But let me make something clear before I go." He lifted my chin.

"If for one minute you try and keep my kids from me, I will take them and you won't see them again." He didn't yell but he did pumped fear in my heart. Could he or would he take

my babies?

****

I hadn't seen Alex since the day at the doctors' office

and that was a week ago. He did hit me up three to four times a

day telling me he was here and if I need anything to let him

know. Of course, it only pissed me off because if he wasn't

here with me, then where was he? I know he's mad but he had

to get over it.

Today I was going to visit my nephew at the hospital.

He was supposed to go home but he ended up getting a slight

infection from the wound so they kept him longer. I took my

shower, got dressed and drove there. I parked in the parking lot

and had to lean on the door to get out.

My stomach was huge, my feet were swollen and I felt

alone in this pregnancy. All of a sudden, I started to cry when I

realized it was my fault. I was so angry with Alex that I kept

him away. This pregnancy was supposed to be fun and he was

supposed to cater to my every need but my pride wouldn't allow me to call him.

"Gabby, is that you?" I heard and turned around.

"Hey Tara. What are you doing here?" I was surprised she was speaking to me. After I found out the reason they hated Zariah, I figure she wouldn't have two words to say.

"Ugh." She stopped speaking and I followed her eyes.

"Hey." I spoke to Alex who had his two bodyguards with him.

"Tara, why did you stop speaking?" I felt Alex grab my hands.

"If you even think for one second about coming for her, I will personally take you out in the ocean and feed you to the sharks."

"ALEX!" I shouted.

"Gabby, she may have portrayed herself as your friend but she had ill intentions. The only reason I'm allowing her to walk out of here is because someone else has plans for her and I made a promise not to touch her."

"What did you do Tara?" She put her head down and attempted to walk away but Alex grabbed her.

"I know you didn't have a big part of how everything went down and you wanted revenge for your father, but you fucked with the wrong family and for that you will die. Now go spend your last days as you wish because it won't be long." He let her arm go and pushed her away from me. We stepped on the elevator and he pulled me in as close as he could. My stomach didn't give us much room.

"I'm sorry for everything Alex. For leaving the house and giving you a hard time when you told me to go home that night. I should've listened to you and not him. I made you miss all the doctors' appointments too. I'm so sorry baby." My face was flooded with tears and he wiped each one away.

"When I'm not here, it doesn't mean, I'm not aware of what's going on. You are going to be my wife and you need to be confident in your spot, or this ain't going to work."

"I know and I will be from now on. You still want me to be your wife?"

"I love you Gabby and no one will ever be my wife but you."

"I love you too." The elevators stopped, the doors opened and neither of us moved as we continued kissing.

"Really!" I looked and AJ was standing there with a frown on his face.

"That's how your ass got pregnant." He said and we all started laughing. Alex and I walked hand in hand into the room. There's no way I was letting him go.

Zariah

Akeem was finally able to come home and of course, I made him stay with me. His mom came over everyday and Akeem would have a fit. He said she was blocking him trying to spend quality time with me. I don't know why he said that when all we did was watch television and eat all day.

I started my residency and on some days I was dead tired but in the end, it would pay off. I'd be Doctor Zariah Martin, well Rowan since we're getting married.

The bullets had him incapacitated for about a week but his horny ass wanted sex almost every day. The good thing about it, was due to this pregnancy, its all I wanted as well. We'd go to bed having sex and wake up to it. When you're young, sex is everything and I'm going to enjoy it as much as possible because once we get older, I'm sure that drive won't be there.

When Akeem found out I was pregnant his ass almost cried. I laugh at him every time we talk about it. He didn't have a problem admitting how happy it made him and if and when I got pregnant again after this one, he'd probably do it again.

In my family we have nothing but thugs, so being with Akeem brings me peace of mind. Yea, he'll get down and dirty if needed but he doesn't make it his business too. Not that other family members do but he's more of a last resort. However, if it comes to his family, or me it's a different story and he will definitely show out.

It feels good to have him cater to me again like he used to. The foot rubs, romantic baths and sexual text messages always brighten up my day; especially when I've had a rough day or week. He was always pushing me to do my best and once we had this baby, I was taking him on a vacation with the four of us, which consisted of me, him, the baby and Jacob.

I had DJ pick him up after I heard what PJ did to Tara. His mom kept him until we both were home and could manage. Now, he was a permanent fixture in our life and I loved him as my own.

****

"Where are you going?" Akeem asked when I came out the bedroom dressed in black. Jacob left with his dad because I let him in on what I had to do. Jacob loved Akeem's father to death. It was funny how he'd fall out to get over to his grandfather.

"Ugh. I'll be back in a few." He came over to me and lifted my face.

"I'm coming."

"You don't even know where I'm going." He smirked.

"Baby, you're dressed in black from head to toe. If it ain't Tara you're going after, I'm sure its someone and I'll be damned if you get hurt again." I smiled and leaned in for a kiss.

I called MJ and asked if she was where he left her and he told me yes. See, Alex wanted to kill her because even though PJ and Tara wanted my family, Gabby's dad is another reason why the shit was happening. I asked him not to get rid of her because after shooting Akeem, she belonged to me. Fortunately for me being his favorite cousin, he didn't touch her.

When she stepped out the hospital, MJ had her snatched up and put away. That was a few days ago and she's been there ever since. Akeem didn't know but I informed him on the way and he wasn't angry. He said he wish I'd let him kill her but he understood why I wanted to do it. It was more than just shooting Akeem. She's hated me from the start and had been plotting for a long time. He parked in front of the place and shut the car off.

"You good?"

"Yup. Are you? If you don't want to watch, I don't mind you sitting in the car."

"Nope. I want to see my ride or die chick/doctor do her thing."

"Oh yea."

"Yup. Make me proud baby." We kissed and got out the car. He held my hand in his and we walked up to the door. Security let us in and the sight before us was disgusting.

"It's about time you got here." Alex said coming out a different room.

187

"Whatever. I had to make sure my man was good first."
I looked at Tara who had shit and piss on her body. Vomit was around her feet and there was a body next to hers.

"Who is that?"

"Oh that her best friend Connie? My cousin Cream killed her for trying to kill CJ and telling PJ where they lived. She started decomposing and Tara here has been vomiting every time she looks at her. Its quite disgusting." Alex laughed and handed me what I needed. I smacked Tara in the face and when she woke up and saw me we heard something dripping on the floor. The bitch had used the bathroom on herself again.

"Tara, you have been a pain in my ass since day one. I tried not to let it bother me but once you came for my fiancé, that's where I draw the line."

"I'm sorry. I swear I am."

"They always are when death is knocking on the door. However, I am going to give you a choice on how you want to die."

"Huh?"

"Well my cousin here has brought me a few things to kill you with. If you want to choose, be my guest."

"Just kill me quick."

"Oh but it won't be fun that way. You see, you bothered me for years and while I may not torture you as long, you will feel my wrath." She didn't say anything.

"Lets see. We have death by acid, death by a machete, death by strangulation or death by being injected with poison."

"Why can't you shoot me?"

POW! I shot her in the knee. I didn't want her dead yet. She screamed like a maniac.

"Ok. Its done. What's next?"

"Zariah, please. I can't take this."

"Too bad." I poured acid on her legs and watched them detach from her body. Morgan gave me the idea. She said it was crazy watching a limb fall off.

I took the machete and chopped off her hands and listened her scream until she passed out. I let a few minutes pass by and tossed water on her to wake up. She opened her eyes and started yelling again. Her voice was barely there.

"This is for shooting my man." I tied the rope tightly around her neck and watched as one of the guys lifted her up by the rope. Her one foot was touching the chair. I stared at her and kicked the chair. She began struggling with the little limbs she had left. Akeem kept his eyes on her until she took her last breath. Alex snapped a picture of him and sent it to someone. His phone rang back and he put it on speakerphone.

"You think I give a fuck about her." I heard through the phone.

"Oh I know you don't but I have a surprise for you." Alex hung the phone up and face timed the person. Another door opened and in came Tara's mom and kids.

"Yo, don't touch my fucking kids." I was now looking at a scared PJ on the phone.

"Zariah, I think its time for you to go." Alex said and asked Akeem to take me home.

"Alex are you?-"

"Don't ask questions you know the answer to." He came close to me.

"All I'm going to say is, he almost killed my kids in Gabby's stomach when he held her there to make sure she got in the accident. His sister almost took your man's life, which would've made your kid grow up without a father."

"I know but.-"

"Sometimes we have to do things to make a point and in this case, its obvious he doesn't give a fuck because he hasn't once pleaded for me not to kill them. He asked me not to touch them but did you here him say he'll take their place?" I shook my head no.

"Exactly! Niggas like him don't need to be here or have their kids grow up to be a replica. You see how he turned out."

"Just like his father." I said and took one last look at PJ on the face time. He had his face turned up but he didn't deny anything Alex said. I couldn't look at the kids because I would feel worse than I already did.

"Call me later Alex." I hugged him and left out. Akeem opened the car door for me.

"Zariah, every action has a reaction."

"I know but."

"You can't feel sorry for a nigga who allowed his kids to be found. If he wanted to protect them, they'd be with him. Instead he left them to fend for themselves. Yes, it's fucked up how they'll meet their fate but they can thank their father for it." I wanted to say something but deep inside he was right. How could PJ bounce and leave his kids? He knows the type of man MJ is and yet, his kids will die because of him.

Alex

"You good baby?" I asked Gabby after they removed my daughter from her stomach. My son came out two minutes ago.

"I can't feel anything but pressure." I kissed her and walked over to see my kids. Both of our moms were in the room watching them clean the twins, weigh them and take their footprints to put on the birth certificates.

"Oh my goodness Alex. Lourdes looks just like you and Alex Jr. looks like Gabby." My mom said wiping her eyes.

It's weird how my daughter resembled me and vice versa with my son. Yea, we named him after me because I wanted to keep my name in the family like my father. It's definitely a lot of juniors. Everyone will eventually get used to it because I'm not changing it.

"Can I see my kids now?" My mom popped me on the back of the head and her mom sucked her teeth. They moved away and let me get close.

I wiped the few tears that slid down my face. I had two mini me's depending on me now besides my wife. Yea, I took Gabby down to the courthouse and we exchanged vows. I didn't want her to birth my kids out of wedlock. Call me old fashioned all you want. Gabby, isn't into material things so she had no problem not having a big wedding. I am going to give her one in a few months though.

"Doctor we need you NOW!" One of the nurses yelled out and all of us ran over to Gabby.

"We need you to step outside." The nurses tried to get us to leave but my ass went over to the bed.

"What the fuck is going on? She was fine." I yelled out and listened to the nurse speak.

"She's bleeding out doctor." I could see tears falling down her face.

"Gabby, listen to me. You're going to be fine." She nodded her head up and down. Her eyes started to close.

"Gabby baby. Keep your eyes open." The monitors were going berserk and so were our parents. Gabby's mom was standing over her kissing her forehead and my mom held her other hand. They were both crying.

"Alex take care of the kids." She was able to whisper.

"Gabby, don't you dare die on me. We've been through too much for you to leave me like this. I need you to fight for me, for the twins you just had." Her grip was getting weaker by the second and I felt myself becoming angrier. I felt a pair of hands on my shoulder and looked up to see my dad and MJ.

"I'm not leaving her." The doctor was yelling and everyone was telling us we had to go because she needed emergency surgery.

"Alex come on so they can operate."

"No! Gabby wake up." I could feel the tears falling down my face. Her dad had to come get her mom and I saw my father walk my mom out. My entire family came here to meet the twins and now their mother may die.

"MJ, I'm not leaving." I could see him getting upset from seeing my face.

"Alex, please come out so they can take her. I know you want her to wake up and she won't if you don't let them do their job. Her pressure is dropping and so is her heart rate." My cousin Zariah said as she stood next to me.

"I will only leave if Zariah stays in here with her." The doctor noticed her scrubs and nametag and agreed to allow her to stay.

"Zariah, don't let them let her die."

"I promise to make sure they do everything to keep her alive; even if I have to do something myself." She hugged me and they pushed Gabby out the room and into another one down the hall. I saw two more doctors and a few nurses headed in the direction Gabby went in.

"She's going to be fine." I heard Arizona's mom say to her dad. She was a daddy's girl so I know it was hurting him too.

We sat in the waiting room for three hours before someone finally came out. The look on Zariah's face was flat and so was the doctors' but they were talking, which in my eyes is a good sign. The doctor told us to give him one minute to find a room to speak in. Zariah ran up and gave me a hug and then Gabby's parents. We followed them in the room and sat down. He introduced himself and gave us a rundown of what was going on.

"Mrs. Rodriquez suffered a ruptured uterus, which is why she began to bleed out. Its similar to a placenta abruption but in her case it was a little more severe. This is known to happen in women who had a cesarean. It can be caused by weak uterine muscles or the use of forceps."

"Were the forceps not sterilized? I don't understand."

"The forceps may have hit something inside her that caused massive bleeding. Unfortunately, tearing some of her uterine wall. She will eventually be able to have kids again before you ask but you should wait at least another year. The longer you wait, the more time you give her to heal. Do you have any questions?"

"Why did it take so long?"

"Because it was so much bleeding we had to cut her more and find where the bleeding was coming from. Once we found it and took care of it we had to make sure there were no more areas affected." He finished telling us.

"You can see her if you'd like. But I have to say she only asked for her dad and husband." Both of us had a grin on our face. I let her dad go in first. He came out ten minutes later and I asked everyone to give me a minute. She was in the room and all of them were going to the nursery to see the babies. My dad had security in there to make sure no one went inside, while we waited to hear about my wife.

"Damn girl, I thought I lost you." She turned to see me and smiled.

"I was so scared Alex. All I could think of was my family, my babies and you. I felt my life slipping away and it wasn't anything I could do." She started crying. I got in bed with her.

"As long as I'm alive, you will always be ok. I know I'm not God but if he would've taken you, I don't know what I would've done."

"Alex, you have to promise me that if anything happened to me, you will be here for the kids."

"I'm not making any promises because nothing is happening to you."

"Alex, please." I looked down at her and gave her the answer she wanted but truth be told, I don't know if I could follow through with the promise. I'm not saying I'd kill myself but I wouldn't be able to take it.

Morgan

"No Le Le." I walked over to the spot her and Camila were in and picked her up.

"Stop hitting your sister." I thought Miguel was playing when he said Le Le hits her a lot but he wasn't. Every chance she got, Camila was getting smacked. I told Miguel to pop her and he almost chewed my ear off. Shit, he didn't have to but I damn sure did. I smacked her hand, but not hard, just as I heard the door close.

"You better not had popped my daughter." He came strolling in from work.

"Well she needs to stop hitting my other daughter." He pecked me on the lips.

"Awwwww come here daddy's girl." I thought he was going for Camila but his petty ass grabbed Le Le and started babying her. I gave him a look and he walked out, leaving me and Camila alone.

After dinner, Miguel helped me get the girls ready for bed but I noticed something was off. I've been feeling it for a while and never said anything. However, today he made it known and if no one else paid attention, I did. I knew him in and out, so when something bothered him, I felt it.

I stepped in the shower and stood in front of him. He stared at me for a few seconds, slid one hand behind my head and kissed me aggressively. Again, another sign. He gets rough when he has a lot on his mind. I love it though.

My arms went around his neck as his other hand groped one of my breasts, making me break our kiss and moan. His mouth latched on to my neck and he began sucking on it slowly; turning me on even more. He pushed me against the wall, lifted one of my legs and forced his way in. I accepted all of him and came so quick; he had to hold me up to make sure I didn't fall from being weak in the knees.

"You love me Morgan."

"Yes baby. Fuck yes." He turned me around, bent me over and dug deep inside. He most likely touched my baby's head from how far he went.

"I can't wait to make you my wife." He pounded away and I let him. He pulled out, turned the water off and led me in the bedroom where we continued.

"I'm not ready to cum yet Morgan. You know I like to be inside you." He moaned out while I rode him.

"Then don't cum." My head was back, his fingers were circling my clit and he used the other hand to guide my hips.

"I can't hold it in any longer. Fuck Morgan. Dammit." He shook a little and I fell on the side of him, still coming down from my own orgasm. He pulled me into him and ran his hand down my face.

"You are so damn beautiful. I promise not to hurt you again." I lifted myself up and stared at him.

"What's going on?" He blew his breath before he spoke.

"I'm thinking about giving my abuela custody of Camila." I smacked him on his chest.

"You will not give my daughter to anyone. What the hell is wrong with you? I thought you wouldn't hurt me anymore." I stood up and grabbed my robe. My eyes started getting watery. I've grown to love her as my own and I'll be damned if he takes her away. I thought he had a bond with her so I wasn't sure where the change came from.

"Morgan I'm not trying to. She isn't a fit with us." He had his arm covering his eyes.

"Why? Because Le Le hits her too much? They are babies; it's what they do. Eventually, Camila will hit her back and you better not say shit when she does."

"That's not it at all Morgan. It's.-" he stopped and ran his hand down his face.

"She reminds you of her mother." He nodded his head. I made my way over to him.

"Miguel, don't let what her mother did tarnish the relationship with your daughter. At the end of the day, she is your flesh and blood. Do you want her growing up as a long lost cousin who finds out her father didn't want her? You know she'll be around the family everyday and start wondering. Miguel, that wouldn't solve anything."

"Morgan, I don't know."

"Baby, I know it's hard; I do." He gave me a look.

"I have to play mom to a child who is supposed to be mine but another woman took that sperm from me. Unfortunately, she got my daughter to come out of her, but I won't allow it to keep me from loving her and you can't either." He didn't say a word.

"I know you love your daughter but it's time you get to know her. I've seen how you've been ignoring her lately and only playing with Le Le. She may not see it now but in due time she will. Both of them deserve the same amount of love. Well the three of them because this one here, is about to shut all of it down." I put his hand on my stomach.

"Miguel, don't allow your son to grow up seeing how you mistreat one of his sisters and adore the other." He popped up.

"You're having my son?" His eyes lit up.

"Yes, I found out today. Here I brought you this." I went to the doctors and had him tell me the sex of the baby. I picked Miguel up a pack of cigars that read; *it's a boy*, along with a pair of baby Jordan's.

"You are forever making me happy. I don't know how to top that." He said laying me down on the bed kissing my stomach.

"You don't have to do anything Miguel. Just don't cheat, or abuse me in any way and I'll always be here for you. I've waited years for you to find your way to me and I'm not giving you up."

"Let's get married next month."

"Baby we can wait. I'm not in a rush and.-"

"You said it's been years and now that we found one another again, why keep waiting. You accepted my proposal, had and will have all my babies and you know how to make Papi moan." He placed kisses on my body and found his way in between my legs.

"Ok baby. We can get married next month. Make me cum one more time. Shitttttt." I came extremely hard and rolled my ass over.

"Yup. Only your husband can make that pussy cum like that." I had to suck my teeth. He was right though. The other two guys I slept with, one being my first, had absolutely nothing on him in the bedroom.

****

"Hey Camila. How is my baby doing?" I picked her up after changing and feeding her. Le Le had the most evil look on her face. I don't care what any of them said. Arcelia Rose Rodriquez is going to be a fucking terror when she gets older.

"I don't know how the girls are doing but Papi is doing very well after that head you gave me." Miguel put his face in the crook of my neck.

"And remember, no one will ever make you feel as good as me." I turned around and he stuck his tongue in my mouth. Camila grabbed his face and started sucking on it. I wish I had a camera to take a picture.

"Looks like I finally have competition." He laughed and took her from me.

I picked Le Le up and she wrapped her arms on my neck. She stared at her father holding Camila. The child was spoiled by him so when she began throwing a fit, I handed her to him. This time when she hit Camila, he said something.

"Morgan can you take Le Le so I can sit with my other daughter for a while?"

"Absolutely baby. We'll be downstairs." He grabbed my free hand and had me sit on his other leg.

"Thanks babe." I gave him a strange look.

"For what?"

"For making me see past the shit her mother did. I was on the verge of saying fuck it, but you made me realize she's not Carlotta."

"You are my husband and when you're upset, it's my job to make you feel better. I know I did that." I kissed the side of his neck.

"You always do. I'll be down in a few." I stood up and walked out the door. I didn't think we were going to make it for a minute but we did and I'm riding with my man until the wheels fall off.

MJ

"What was his reaction after you finished?" I asked my brother Alex, who was sitting across from me at my office. He and Gabby had come home yesterday with the twins, after being in the states for a month.

"Honestly, he had this attitude the entire time until he saw their bodies drop. Then he started cursing and popping shit. Maybe he didn't believe I'd do it." He shrugged his shoulders as he finished giving me the details of what went down with PJ. We had been so wrapped up in other things I forgot to ask.

I know people think we ain't shit for killing kids but it's killed or be killed. He wasn't thinking about my niece and nephew when he set Gabby up for the accident. Nor were they thinking about my daughter Le Le when the plan was to kidnap Morgan at my crowning.

"Fuck it. Baako is coming in today with a treat so meet me at the spot later. Nigel hasn't eaten in a week. You know

how much you get a kick out of Nigel taking people's lives."
He laughed and stood up.

"What time is my nieces party tomorrow?"

"Man, I don't know. Morgan has all types of shit going on and your mother isn't making it any better. She rented the damn football field at the high school."

"WHAT?"

"Morgan talking about, *"Let's have a small circus/ carnival for them."* I said mocking her.

"FUCK! That means Gabby is going to want the same shit. Who the hell wants to deal with that?"

"Excuse me Mr. Rodriquez, your cousin DJ is on the line." I told Alex to hold on while I took the call.

DJ wanted to make sure we had a car waiting when he got to the airport later. Him and Savannah were coming before everyone else. He said they were driving him crazy because his girl is pregnant with twins as well, which we expected since she's one. We don't know where Alex twins came from but it's in our bloodline now.

"I see you have mostly men working here?" Alex said and started laughing hard as hell.

"Fuck you."

"Don't get mad at me because you got caught. Morgan ain't playing no games with you huh?"

"No I'm not and the only women working here are the ones old enough to be his grandmother or they'll be relatives." My girl came in to bring me lunch.

"Hey sis." She handed me my bag and gave him a hug.

"Look at you Alex. All sexy and shit."

"I know right. Maybe one day you and I can slip away from him and Gabby."

"Alex, I will fuck you up in here. And Morgan you keep entertaining his ass." I took the top off my soda.

"I'm just saying bro. Why not keep it in the family?" I jumped out my seat fast as hell. They thought the shit was hysterical until I pulled my fucking gun out.

"MIGUEL!" Alex shook his head.

"We were just playing." Morgan tried to keep me calm.

"Oh you playing now huh? Everything's a fucking joke til somebody gets killed." I started cursing Alex out in Spanish.

"I'm out sis. Remember it's a date."

"Oh you still playing nigga?" He hauled ass out my office.

I turned around and Morgan was in the chair removing her shirt. She stood up and let her pants hit the floor. Her lace panty set looked sexy as hell on her, even with my son in her belly.

"You ain't getting none. Go find Alex." I moved past her and sat down to eat my lunch.

"Oh I can have him, now that you made him leave."

"I'm over the jokes Morgan. I swear, I'll kill your ass today." She came closer and sat on my lap facing me. I reached behind her to grab my drink.

"I'm serious Morgan. You ain't getting.-" She let the bra drop to the floor and her breasts were in my face. She started rubbing on them and moaning. My dick grew hard as hell.

"You play too much." I stood her up and went to lock the door.

"What are you going to do about it?" She let her panties fall to the floor.

"Nothing. You want it, you take it." I smirked as she moved towards me.

"You ok with that?" I know she asked because of the shit with Carlotta.

"You are the only woman I'd let take anything from me without my consent."

"I guess you do love me." She unbuckled my jeans.

"More than you can ever know." I ran my hand through her hair as she did what she does best.

****

"What up Baako? Long time no see." I greeted him when he pulled up to the spot. He gave Alex a man hug as well as DJ, who came in an hour ago and decided to roll with us. AJ wanted to come but my sister made his ass stay with her.

"I'm not dead and my mother is the one behind all this bullshit, so I can't complain." He said in the best English he

214

could. His broken English gets on my nerves but he good peoples.

"If I thought for one minute you were with her, you already know." He nodded. I trusted Baako but kept an eye on him just in case. He may not be fucking with Akeena but she's still his mother.

"Anyway, what you got for me?" I rubbed my hands together and walked in the other room with all of them.

"I know you've been looking for him and being you're unaware of what he looks like, I brought him to you." None of us knew who he spoke of and waited for him to take the pillowcase off his head.

"Who the fuck is he?" DJ asked tossing water on him. The dude was in the chair looking to be half dead.

"Oh this is Armond. He is the one who saved my mother from the whore house and plotting to take y'all out."

"Oh he is huh?" I stared to see if I knew him from anywhere.

"Alex, can you get Nigel and Farrah?"

"I swear to God Alex, I will shoot your ass if you play today." DJ had his gun ready. He still hasn't gotten over my brother sicking Nigel on him from the last time.

"Scary ass." Alex loved seeing people scared.

"Who the hell is Farrah?" Baako asked and looked at my cousin who shrugged his shoulders.

"Wait until you see her cuz."

"OH SHIT!" Baako yelled out and moved out the way.

"Hold up. You went and got another one? You sick as hell MJ." DJ shook his head.

"Farrah here is not a Python. She is a green anaconda and there's a difference. I had her shipped here from the Amazon a few months ago. She is as pretty as Nigel, don't you think?" And before anyone talks shit? It's not the size of the one on those dumb ass movies. She is rather big and long though.

"What is up with you and these snakes?"

"The way I see it is, if I let the snakes get them, their death won't be by my hands."

"You know that makes no sense right? You're the one putting the snakes on them." DJ said.

"But am I the one actually killing them though?" They all busted out laughing and I shrugged my shoulders. It did sound crazy but fuck it.

"Tell me your crazy ass don't have a fucking leash on the snake." Baako said making me turn around.

"Really Alex." He had a fucking long ass orange extension cord wrapped around her neck. I don't know when he put it on her but it looked crazy.

"Say what you want but this is a big bitch and I need total control of her." Baako was laughing so hard, he had tears coming out. DJ had his gun pointed at Farrah.

"Alright y'all. We have to be serious." I had to contain my laughter. I made Baako get a picture because no one was going to believe this shit.

"What do you want?" Armond said finally opening his eyes.

"Oh shit. The dead had arisen." I said and walked back over to Armond.

"Back to you. Where's the bitch you're working with?" We all stopped laughing and watched Nigel slither his way over.

"I'm not giving her up so go ahead and kill me."

"See this the shit I be talking about. Niggas want me to kill them quickly but it's not fun that way. I'm telling you it's way better watching the life slip away as his bones get crushed."

"Whoa Farrah!" We all turned around fast as hell.

"Yooooo. She trying to eat so I suggest everyone move out the way." Alex let the cord go. DJ and Baako jumped on the table.

Nigel had already wrapped himself around Armond as Farrah went over and basically did the same thing. You could hear his bones crush as both snakes literally squeezed the life out of him. Blood was coming from his mouth and I guess Farrah smelled it. She tried repeatedly to eat him but it didn't work. I had Alex pull her back and let Pablo come in to chop his body up and leave it on the ground. All I can say is, Farrah should be full for a while and Pablo didn't have much to clean.

"Yo, if you ever have to kill me, shoot my ass. That right there is worse than anything I've ever seen." Baako said and both him and DJ jumped off the table.

"LOOK OUT!" Alex yelled and they hauled ass out the room.

"Your cousin dumb as hell bro and so is your employee. We not even in the same room anymore and they still running." Both of us couldn't do shit but laugh. We never went back in after Pablo cut Armond up and watched Farrah eat him on the camera. I couldn't wait to go home and tell Morgan this shit.

Gabby

"Alex is going to be mad but I'm definitely having a party for my babies like this." I told Brea as we sat at one of the tables. It was MJ's twins' birthday party. His mom had a full-blown carnival, circus and petting zoo out here.

"Shit, you better learn how to control that fucking attitude and mouth first." His cousin Ricky said and gave me a fake smile. I didn't really know him personally but we've spoken on occasions.

"You don't even know me." He looked me up and down before speaking.

"I don't have to. Believe it or not, I'm tight with all my cousins; especially MJ and Alex. I know shit you don't even know. You sitting here with your cousin acting like you're better than everyone out here." My mouth hit the floor.

"No I'm not."

"Bitch bye."

"Bitch." Now I was pissed.

"Damn right I called you a bitch. My cousin has been caught up in so much shit behind your ass."

"What are you talking about?" Brea was sitting there shaking her head.

"First off... the nonsense with your ex, who you allowed to keep you in a spot for a certain amount of time, in order for someone to almost kill you, is ridiculous. You should've never entertained that nigga, knowing you had a man. Then the two of you lose a baby, only for you to stop speaking to him and give him your ass to kiss. By the way, I told him to say fuck you." He smirked.

"Anyway, your entire pregnancy you made motherfuckers think he didn't want his kids, all because you thought he was messing with his ex. My cousin missed out on the pregnancy because of this bitch ass attitude you got." He stepped closer to me and Brea stood up to get in the middle. I guess he did know a lot.

"This tough charade you're putting up and trying to be a boss isn't going to do anything but make you lose him." I sucked my teeth.

"Now I'm all for being a strong woman and not catering to a fuck boy. It's too many chicks out here who fall victim to some good dick. However, you're going about it wrong and my cousin ain't one of those niggas who takes kindly to the shit you're doing." By now I was beyond mad and the next thing out my mouth was hurtful but it was all that came to mind at the moment.

"Why are you coming for me? And you're a dude at that. What man does this bitch shit you're doing? You want to be a chick so bad, that you'll start shit with them just to make you feel better?" He tossed his head back laughing and then smacked the shit out of me. My head spun by how hard he hit me. I went to swing but Brea stopped me.

"ALEX!!!" I heard Brea yell.

"Bitch don't ever in your motherfucking life disrespect me." I saw Mateo pull Ricky back and then Brea. She was pregnant and shouldn't have been in the middle of us anyway.

"What the fuck is going on?" Alex and a bunch of the other guys came running over. I saw a guy go over to Ricky and figured it was his man by the way he spoke.

"I was sitting here and this dude, she man or whatever." I waved my hand towards Ricky.

"Gabby, I'm telling you right now to watch your fucking mouth. All that is uncalled for." Alex said making me give him a crazy look.

"What? He smacks me and you're cursing at me. Are you serious right now?" I felt tears coming down my face.

"Oh you thought because he put two kids in you, he would allow you to treat his family members like shit? Think again stupid."

"That's enough Ricky."

"Fuck you, him and whoever else has something to say. And for the record RICKY!" I made sure to put an emphasis in his name.

"I'm not a weak bitch and neither him or you will make me feel like I have to bow down for us to be together. I don't need Alex or none of this bullshit."

"Say what you want but you heard what I said bitch. I will lay you the fuck out if you hurt him again."

"Gabby. I need to ask you something and be honest with your answer because it will make or break this relationship." Alex said after grabbing my arm.

"What?"

"Are you homophobic?"

"No but.-"

"But nothing. If you're not, then why did you call him out his name? She man or whatever he is, is what you called him." I didn't even realize he paid attention but I guess he did.

"I was mad because he called me a bitch and.-"

"I understand and I'm definitely going to handle that. Whether he felt that way or not, it was wrong but you were just as wrong. Not only that, you're out here going back and forth while our kids are here."

"I'm sorry."

Why didn't you say something when he first came over here?" He moved my hair out my face.

"Alex I don't need you to protect me all the time."

"I didn't say you did but I damn sure don't need my girl fighting my cousin. But as your man, I'm going to do it regardless. However, this is my nieces party and both of you are acting their age."

"I'm over this shit." I started walking away.

"Where are you going?"

"I'm taking my kids and.-"

"Think again Gabby."

"Huh?"

"I don't give a fuck how mad you are, my kids are staying right here."

"No they're not." I tried to walk off and he snatched me by my arm.

"You are really fucking testing me Gabby. In all this time I've known you, I've let you get away with a lot of shit. Shit, no one else would. I swear it's taking everything in me right now not to put my hands on you and I don't hit women."

"But you'll hit me."

"I'm not trying to and I'm containing myself. Look. If you want to leave then go. We'll be home later."

"I'm not leaving."

"At this point it's no longer a question if you want to leave or not. It's time for you to go." I stood there with my arms folded.

"GET THE FUCK OUT OF HERE!" He yelled and it was as if all eyes were on us. I saw my brother coming to where we were, along with Joy and my niece.

"Alex." I reached out for him but he snatched his arm away.

"Don't touch me."

"Alex, I'm sorry."

"Don't say another fucking word to me. Matter of fact, pack your shit and go back to the states. I will bring the kids during the week. I can't stand to be around you right now." He walked off and left me standing there.

"What happened? Are you ok?" My brother asked and I started explaining what went down. Joy had an evil look on her face as she looked at Ricky, who flipped her the finger.

"Gabby I'm sorry my cousin spoke to you that way. He is very protective of MJ and Alex as you can see."

"I just want to go."

"I'll take her Joy. Stay here with everyone."

"Are you sure? I can go with you."

"Yea. I'll see you at the house." He kissed her and she began walking off.

"It's ok AJ. I'll have one of the security dudes take me." At first he gave me a hard time but after he saw I wouldn't give in, he walked me to the car. I gave him a hug and asked the driver to take me to a hotel. I refused to stay in the house or go back to the states without my kids. Plus, my parents would kill me.

I checked into a hotel in San Juan and had them put me in a room overlooking the ocean. It was beautiful and it gave me time to think about what Ricky said. He was right when he said since I had been so weak for PJ; I refused to be that way again and gave Alex a hard time because of it.

Well he didn't say it in those words but I read between the lines. Alex is good to me and I don't appreciate him like I should. Not that Alex was making me weak but I was taking it out on him. I gave him my ass to kiss many times and he never gave up on me. I sat in the room for hours crying to myself.

It was after midnight and I missed him and my babies. Every night we'd both sit in the room with them and watch them sleep before going to bed. We hadn't had sex since I delivered but being under him, was enough. Of course thoughts of him sleeping with another chick began to cloud my mind. I tossed and turned all night when I finally decided to call and check on them. I face timed him thinking he wouldn't answer but he did.

"They're fine." He answered showing the both of them sleep in the crib.

"Alex."

"Goodbye Gabby." He disconnected the call. I slammed my phone on the nightstand and laid there staring at the ceiling. At least I know he was alone but then again he wasn't in the room.

"What? It's four in the morning. Are you dying?" He asked when I called him back.

"No Alex. I miss you and our kids."

"Whose fault is that?" I noticed he wasn't saying my name.

I had to think of a way to get him to say it or tell me he love me. That way, I'd know if a chick was there and even if it were, she'd know about me. Before I responded the phone hung up. A few seconds later he face timed me.

"Look Gabby. I'm tired and my kids get up early. There is no bitch in the bed with me, in my bathroom or anywhere else in this house. You know, no one comes on this estate." *Shit he caught me.*

"Alex that's not why.-"

"Yes it is. If I wanted a chick here, I could, but I would never disrespect you or my kids like that. What type of nigga you think I am?" He was so angry with me that the venom was rolling off his tongue like it was nothing.

"You need to grow the fuck up Gabby and that's on some real shit. You're insecure, petty, childish and play too many games." I found myself trying to apologize again but he shut it down.

"You want to be a boss bitch but go running at the first sign of trouble. So what Ricky smacked you? You should've kicked him in the dick or hooked off. I wouldn't have been mad and he damn sure would've respected you more. Instead you run away, cry and proceed to take my kids. Then you get mad at me like I'm the one who did it." I wiped my eyes as he continued to go in on me.

"I love the hell out of you Gabby. You're my wife, you birthed my son and daughter and sex me real good but what's all that, when you still play teenage games? Call me when you grow up, until then, we'll co-parent. Peace." He disconnected the call again.

Damn! I wonder if he'll divorce me?

****

"I'll see you when I get back." I kissed both of my babies on the cheek.

I had been staying at the hotel all week and coming to his house during the day to be with the kids. He didn't come home until after ten every night, which is fine because it gave me time to be with my babies. We didn't speak at all and if we did, it was to say hello, goodbye or discuss the kids. This must be what it feels like to co-parent.

"Bye Alex." I walked out the house and closed the door. I walked over to the car Morgan was in. She told him she'd take me to the airport instead of riding with security. They'd be behind us but I wouldn't be in the car with them.

"Abuela, already has the place ready for when you come back." I heard Alex say as I opened the car door. I decided to stay over there until I get my own place. Its easier for him to see the kids and before anyone talks shit, this was my plan prior to the shit with his cousin and us breaking up.

"Ok." He wanted me to stay in one of the houses on the estate but those houses were for his siblings, plus I refused to see another woman going in and out his place.

"Gabby." I rolled the window down further. He came closer to the car and kneeled on my side of the door.

"I'm going to wait for you to grow up. I want my wife here like she's supposed to be." I let a smile creep on my face.

"Don't take forever." He leaned in the car and kissed my lips. I grabbed the back of his head and slipped my tongue in. I almost got out but he wouldn't let me.

"I'll see you when you come back." He said and backed away.

"Girl, he ain't going nowhere. Stop looking pitiful."

"I don't know Morgan. He was pretty mad at the party. Oh, I'm sorry about the drama."

"Its fine. Ricky is a piece of work but his heart is always in the right place."

"Did he do you the same way?" I asked waiting for an answer.

"HELL NO! Ricky knows I don't play that shit. Miguel would beat his ass if he ever came at me sideways."

"Well, I guess its different with Alex."

"Look Gabby. I don't know why he came for you the way he did, but Alex and MJ are like his brothers. Alex was upset at what you were taking him through and Ricky didn't appreciate it. He shouldn't have approached you the way he did and I'm sure Alex had no idea he was. However, you should've called him over there. Regardless of who was wrong, Alex would've never allowed him to speak to you like that. Then you treat Alex like shit in front of his family and to be honest, I had to get MJ to hold his mother back."

"WHAT?"

"What did you expect? He is her child no matter how old he is. Gabby you can't go around thinking you're better than anyone or even portraying yourself as a boss."

"But I wasn't."

"You were and you made Alex feel like shit. How would you feel if he treated you like that in front of everyone?

236

If you want to keep him, I suggest you get it together before its

too late."

"You said he wasn't going anywhere."

"He's not, right now. But if you keep acting the way

you do, he'll leave." I nodded my head and sat quiet for the

remainder of the ride to the airport. I have to get my man back

and I'm going to start the minute I return.

PJ

I rushed to the states after watching that sick bastard murder my kids. I really didn't care much for my mother because she raised me to be hateful and evil to others. My father cheated on her with Zariah's mom, even though her mother had him first and he was basically the cheater.

Then he beat my mom the same way he did all his women, I'm assuming, left her to find this Heaven chick again and ended up losing his life over her. I'm not saying a woman won't have you lose yourself because Lord knows I have with Gabby.

I loved that woman with all my heart and wished like hell I did a better job at being her man. She was the perfect person for me but I was young and couldn't get past my cheating ways. We all know when chicks see you have someone, they really press. Connie was a creep who got pregnant and kept the baby. I met Gabby, made her my girl and continued messing with Connie.

Eventually, it started to come out and thoughts of my girl leaving me drove me in a rage and I laid hands on her a few times. My mom said it was ok because some women needed to know their place. However, watching Gabby cry told me my mom was ok with what my pops did to her.

She was supposed to be my wife and carry my kids, not the fuck nigga who took my kids. Yea, I know she married him right before delivering her twins. Shit, I thought after the first miscarriage, she'd leave him alone. Nope; it pushed them closer and I hated it.

I guess I'm to blame when it comes to my kids dying too. The day I left my moms house I should've taken them with me. Instead, I hopped the first flight and was out. I knew the type of niggas the Rodriquez's were and never thought for one minute my choices would affect them. I found their bodies in shallow graves in the back of my house.

Yea, those niggas don't give a fuck about anyone and the cops definitely don't see or hear shit when it comes to them. That's why I'm going to take something special away from them. Well, Alex anyway.

"How you been Gabby?" I asked when she closed the back door to her car. I noticed her body freeze up and knew I had her.

"What are you doing here?" We were standing outside the mall.

"Ugh, it's a public place. Why wouldn't I be?"

"I didn't think I'd see you again that's all." She shrugged her shoulders and opened the driver side to her door.

"Listen, I want to talk to you. Can we go somewhere and talk?"

"PJ, you know as well as I, that it's not a good idea. I shouldn't even be conversing with you now."

"I never took you for the one to be controlled by a man."

"PJ, he's not controlling me but the last time we spoke, you set me up to be involved in a car accident. I could have died. I'm moving to Puerto Rico so he can keep me safe. I don't know what's going on but my kids are my main priority."

"I know and I'm sorry. I was pissed you chose him. Come on. We used to be friends Gabby." I saw how she was fighting with her decision.

"Ok but I can only stay for a few minutes."

"That's all I need." I told her to follow me. I noticed she didn't have any security, which was odd, but better for me. I planned on asking what that's about.

I parked in front of my house that she or no one knew of. I had it for a year and never stayed here. It was a gift for Connie's birthday but she isn't here either, so it was sitting here unoccupied. CJ had no problem telling me where to find her body either. Someone placed it in a garbage bin behind one of the projects. I never went to claim it because honestly, what was I going to do with it.

"This is nice PJ. When did you get it?" She asked after we stepped in the house.

"A while ago. Let me show you around." I took her hand in mine and she didn't resist. I showed her each room and stopped in the bedroom.

"Wait until your kids see it. They are going to love their rooms." She stood in front of the window.

"They won't." She turned around quickly and came over to me.

"Why not? Are you and your baby mama on the outs again?" That's when I knew she had no idea what her man did. I held her face in mine and saw nothing but her innocence.

"Where are your bodyguards?"

"They were with me at the mall but I told them to meet me at my house."

"And they listened?"

"Yea, why wouldn't they? I'm not beefing with anyone and to be honest, I don't like them following me around anyway." She shrugged her shoulders as if it were nothing.

"I miss you Gabby." I kissed her lips and felt a push to my chest.

"PJ, this is not why I'm here. You asked to talk so talk." I stared at her.

"I'm leaving." She started to walk out. I snatched her wrist and her entire body jerked.

242

"PJ, what are you doing? Let go."

"I can't do that Gabby." I pushed her against the wall, kissed her neck and massaged her breasts.

"Stop it. What's wrong with you?" She smacked the hell out of me and that was all it took for me to turn into my father.

"Bitch." I punched her in the face and watched her body fall to the ground. She laid there unconscious.

I took her clothes off, laid her on the bed and snapped a few pictures. Most of them were from the back and I had a few with my face in between her legs. I'm no rapist and didn't violate her but I made sure to get some photos in compromising positions.

After I finished, I threw her clothes back on and carried her to the basement. I attached the chains on both of her legs, laid her on the mattress I had there and stared. I could let her go but I'm going to make sure the nigga thinks we're together.

Send! A few minutes later my phone rang.

"Where is she?" He roared in the phone.

"Oh she's in the shower. We just finished fucking again."

"I don't believe you."

"I know you saw the photos nigga. What am I lying for?" He remained quiet.

"PJ, where are you?" Gabby said quietly but loud enough for him to hear.

"Oh yea. Tell her to stay over there and she better hope I let her see my kids. Trifling ass bitch." He hung up. She tried to get up and realized her legs were chained.

"What the hell? PJ please let me go." The crying and whining began.

"Nope. He's going to feel the pain from killing my kids." She covered her mouth.

"Yea, he killed my entire family and trust me when I say your time is coming."

"I don't have anything to do with that."

"Neither did my kids." I walked up the steps and listened to her yell. I wanted to let her free but it felt good being in control of the situation. Alex may have said fuck her,

244

but after a few days, I know he'll come looking for her; even if

it's to curse her out personally. She'll be dead by then, so he

better get her grave ready now.

Akeena

"I haven't heard from him PJ. I think something happened." I said in the phone. Armond was supposed to go over to the states a few weeks ago to kidnap Zariah. I haven't heard from him since the day he walked out the door.

"I don't know what to tell you Akeena. I do know those motherfuckers killed my entire family." I remained quiet on the phone as I listened to him go in detail about watching his family die.

"I'm sorry PJ. I had no idea."

"It's all good. I have something of Alex's that I can guarantee he'll come running to get."

"I don't see him coming for anything. I mean it's.-"

"Oh he'll come for her."

"Her. Who do you have?"

"Gabriela Rowan."

"No shit. How the fuck did you pull that off?" I had a
big grin on my face.

"I have my ways. If you want your revenge before I
take her life, I suggest you get over to the states ASAP." He
hung up and I booked my flight just that fast. I couldn't believe
we finally had someone of value or should I say leverage to use
against them.

The flight to the US took forever but it would be worth
it when I found Armond and laid eyes on Gabby. Her family
and the extended one has caused nothing but drama in my life
and it's time to return the favor. The pilot came over the
intercom and told us to unfasten our seat belts and remain
seated until the attendants told us what to do. Once they let us
off, I was on my way to PJ.

I waited for my luggage and stared at everyone;
paranoid that someone would recognize me. No one knew what
I looked like but Gabby's parents and uncles. I did get some

247

facial surgery done but some may still know who I am. I grabbed my things, headed for the door and waved down a cab to get in.

When the driver pulled up to the address; I hesitated to get out. Instead my ass called PJ on the phone. The street only had a few houses on it. He stepped out onto the porch and my body reacted. I can't lie; him and his brother are sexy as hell. I opened the door to step out and he assisted with my luggage. I paid the driver and followed him inside. It was pretty decent and it seemed as if no one was here but him.

"You look sexy as fuck Akeena." He gave me a hug and his hands moved down to my ass.

"Thanks. Where is she?" I tried to move from his embrace but he kept me there. He leaned in to kiss me and I turned my head.

"Stop acting like you don't want to." He lifted me on the counter, spread my legs and put his face in my pussy. I didn't even try to stop him.

"Right there PJ. Oh shit. Yessss." I screamed out and continued riding his face until I had two more. He lifted his head and wiped his chin.

"Can I fuck you?" I was still coming down from my high when I felt him plunge inside.

"This pussy tight as hell." PJ was fucking the hell out of me on the counter.

"Make that ass clap for me." He said after grabbing me down and turning me around. I wasn't trying to keep this fiasco going but there's no way I was making him stop.

"Yea Akeena. I see why my brother was strung. Your old ass got that snap back pussy." He smacked my ass and I squirted all over him. The two of us fucked for well over an hour and a bitch was tired. We ended up taking a shower and falling asleep.

****

I woke up to somebody screaming. PJ was on the side of me still knocked out. I stepped out the bed and opened the bedroom door cautiously. I didn't see anyone and headed towards the screams. The door to what I'm assuming is the basement, was cracked. I walked down the steps and came face to face with the one and only, Miss Gabriela Rowan.

"It's funny how you're in the same situation your mother was." I smiled and glanced around the room. Both of her ankles were chained to the wall and all she had on was a t-shirt and shorts. Her hair was all over and you could see the bags in her eyes from crying.

"Then you know my man will find me or better yet, my father will. I mean he did rescue my mom." When she said that, the memories came rushing back.

"Its going to be hard when no one knows your missing." PJ did tell me before we dosed off that she came to the states to pack for her move to Puerto Rico. Evidently she was moving with her baby daddy.

"Who are you and why are you working with him?"

"I'm your worst nightmare." I punched her in the face repeatedly. She tried to fight back but with the chains attached it was hard. With each hit, all I thought of was the abuse I suffered being thrown in that whorehouse.

"Please stop." I heard her cry out.

"I'm going to make you suffer for your parents sins." I kicked her in the stomach, back and anywhere else I could. By the time I finished she had blood coming from her face, and head.

I guess she wasn't a fighter after all. I left her there, went upstairs to shower and made some breakfast. My stomach was growling as the eggs and bacon cooked on the stove. PJ came behind me and wrapped his arms around my waist. His hand went inside my pants and I became drenched by his touch. Shit, I couldn't tell you whose sex was the best between him and his brother but right now, I'm going to enjoy his.

I've been over here for a few days now and Armond

has yet to surface. In the meantime, me and Gabby have been

getting acquainted with one another. PJ didn't care what I did,

as long as she stayed alive. Yesterday, I cut all her hair off and

made her eat food off the ground. I only fed her bread and

water, which is the minimum to keeping a person alive.

"Good morning." The person said on the phone when I

answered.

"What do you want?"

"You." The way he said it, sent chills down my spine.

MJ had a voice that made you believe he really is the

boogeyman.

"Then why haven't you found me yet?"

"I'm coming for you and PJ." I stopped walking

upstairs and turned around. I made my way down the steps,

looked out the window and checked the house.

252

"Don't get quiet now."

"Goodbye." I hung up and he called back.

I turned the phone off and went to lie down. I had no choice but to leave the states. If they knew PJ and I were together, most likely they knew where we were. I jumped up, went downstairs, wrote a note to leave on the counter and then to the basement to check on Gabby.

"I had fun missy but its time for me to go." I had her face in my hand. One of her eyes were swollen shut and her body was bruised badly.

"You really should get yourself together. Tonight PJ plans on having some of his good pussy as he says." I could see her face turn up.

"Please help me."

"Help you." I laughed.

"I wanted to kill you but he wouldn't allow it. I hope you and everyone else die a painful and slow death. I hate all of you." I spit in her face and hit her one more time before leaving. I stood up and stopped in my tracks when I saw him standing there.

MJ

"He has her." Alex yelled and threw his phone.

We were sitting at my house watching a game when his notifications went off. His face was turned up and when he called the person back, it was as if he turned into someone else. I wasn't sure what were in the photos because he wouldn't show me, which most likely meant they were bad.

"What happened?" I needed to know for sure what went down before my next move. He began telling me about the photos and what the conversation was about. I heard some of it when he was on the phone but not enough to put it all together until he filled me in.

"What I'm about to ask you is not something you may want to hear but we have to be sure." He looked at me.

"By any chance, do you think she's there at her own free will?"

"Nah. I heard her in the background asking for him but not the way you think." I could tell in his face the shit was bothering him.

"I'm going to find out what the fuck is really up. " he said and tossed back the beer he was drinking.

"I thought you told him to tell her not to come home."

"I did but what if she's doing it for my attention?"

"Huh?" Now I was confused as hell.

"I need to make him think, I believe she wants him and not come for her. That way, when I go there, he won't expect it." I nodded and called my mom and asked if she could come get his kids. Alex was bugging and needed to go get her.

"Tell ma never mind." I gave him a crazy look and did what he asked.

"What's that about?"

"I'll go over in a day or two."

"Alex."

"Nah MJ. I told her to make sure she has security wherever she goes and if he has her, then she didn't listen. I'm going to let her ass stay there and think about her actions."

"You don't think he'll hurt her."

"Nope. He loves her too much, plus he would have never sent me those pictures."

"I don't know Alex. You did take away his family."

"PJ is scary MJ. Even if he did want to kill her, he wouldn't be the one doing it." I sat there thinking if I could do the same if it were Morgan but then again we didn't have the issues in our relationship like him and Gabby.

He stayed over a little longer and took the kids home. Morgan came in the house a little after nine after being over my sisters house half the day with the girls. She asked me to help her get them ready for bed.

After the girls were asleep, Morgan got in the tub. I thought about getting in with her but she seemed to be enjoying the peace and quiet. I walked on the other side, took a shower and got out.

"Why aren't we married yet?" She asked coming out the bathroom with her towel wrapped around.

"I'm waiting on you."

"I've been ready."

"So what you wanna do? Shit, we can get married in the morning." I removed the towel and began putting lotion on her.

"Can we do it tomorrow and have my wedding after your son comes? I still want my big wedding but I don't want to go into labor walking down the aisle or even the day before. And my wedding dress won't fit with this belly." She rubbed it.

"Its whatever you want baby. I'll marry you everyday if its what you wanted." She smiled and pulled my face close to hers.

"I am the luckiest woman in the world." I had to smile.

"Why is that?" I placed her in the bed naked. We both slept like this and kept our clothes on the side, in case we had to get up quick.

"Because my man is perfect." I gave her the side eye. I wouldn't say I was perfect because we did go through some things. I did want to hear why she thought it though.

"You are to me. Yes, we had a few issues but so does all relationships. However, your one mishap is partly my fault. I told you it was over and to leave me alone. I'm not saying you should've slept with her but its not fair to hold it against you." I was shocked to hear her speaking this way.

"You protect your family and put me in my place when needed. I love the way you make love to me, kiss me, and how you keep yourself grounded with everything going on. You may not be perfect to others but Miguel; you are all that and more to me. I love you so much." And here comes the waterworks from her.

"Morgan you, my girls, my son and all my future kids are my life and will remain that way forever. I just want you to be sure about becoming one with me. There's no out's once you have my last name."

"I'm positive."

"Listen to me." I made her stare at me.

"I'm saying this because my job is hectic as you know and there will be a lot more times where I come home angry. Its things you won't know and can't know."

"Miguel, I've been around through a lot already and I'm still here. The only thing that will make me leave you, is if you cheat or abuse me. I won't tolerate that and you can try to stay in my life all you want but that's where I draw the line." She gave me a serious look.

"I will never put my hands on you and as far as cheating, no one will have me but you. I've been there and done that with women so that part of my life is over. All I want is you." I pecked her lips.

"Now if you ever want a threesome with another woman, I can set it up." I smirked and she smacked me on the arm.

"I am selfish with you and will never watch you give another woman pleasure."

"I'm saying though Morgan. She can do you, I can watch and.-"

"HELL NO." She shut it down fast.

"You're mine and only mine." She began to get mad.

I had to laugh at her spoiled ass. I wouldn't allow another woman or man to touch her anyway. I wanted to see where her head was at and her answer gave me the confirmation I needed.

"And you're mine. No other man can make that pussy cum the way I do." She sucked her teeth as I pried her legs opened.

"They damn sure can't. Ssssss." She moaned out. I gave my future wife multiple pleasures and she did the same.

The next day she was up before me getting the kids dressed. I asked her what was the rush and she almost chewed my ear off. She said the reverend was on his way and I better get ready.

I got a kick out of how angry she was. Her face would turn up, she'd roll her eyes and her eyebrows would arch almost in a unibrow. I started the shower and prepared myself to make Morgan my wife.

"Hey Mrs. Rodriquez." I kissed her after the reverend pronounced us husband and wife. We were married at ten o clock in front of my siblings, daughters, nieces and nephew. I thought Morgan would be upset because her family wasn't here but she wasn't. I planned on calling them last night and sending the jet but by the time we finished having sex, we both fell asleep.

"Mr. Rodriquez. I think our honeymoon should start when everyone leaves." She whispered in my ear and my dick grew. She walked away laughing. I heard someone clear their voice and it was my father.

"Congratulations son."

"Thanks pops. Did you get ma pregnant again?" We looked over and she was all teary eyed. He shrugged his shoulders and left me standing there.

"How is ma even still allowed to have kids?" Alex said and we both started laughing.

"I don't know but Morgan is going to be the same way."

"And so is Gabby." We gave each other a pound.

The day went by quickly with everyone staying at my house after our quick ceremony. My mom took the girls with her and my wife and I definitely had our honeymoon in the house, on the balcony, outside by the pool and in the garage. She wanted to have sex in the front yard but claimed her belly was too big and it didn't feel right. I told her the pool is outside but she said its different. Who knows?

****

"She's here." The person said in the phone.

262

"I'm on the way." I sent a text to Alex and told him to get ready. I hung up, put my phone on the nightstand and sat up in the bed. I left Morgan lying there and quietly walked in the bathroom to get ready. This shit is finally about to be over.

"You ok." Morgan asked stepping in with me.

"I am now." She smiled.

"Why is that?" Her hands were bringing my man to life.

"Because you're in here. Shittttt." She kneeled down and had my ass moaning too loud if you ask me. Fuck it, my wife could get that.

"My grandmother is coming to stay with you until I return." I told her, speaking of my moms mom.

"Good. She'll cook for me." Morgan smiled and laid back in the bed.

"My entire family spoils you."

"I know right."

"That's how I know you were the woman meant to be in my life." I kissed her.

"Go baby before you get something started and.-" She couldn't finish because Alex was ringing the doorbell. He's the only one who rings it that much to let us know he's coming. Ricky told him how he walked in on us having sex and Alex said he refused to ever see some shit like that.

"Yo. Is Morgan dressed?" He asked on the outside of the door.

"Yea." He opened it and went over to her. She stood up, hugged him and he rubbed her belly.

"This is a big nigga in here." Morgan smacked his arm.

"Don't call my baby that."

"Why not. MJ calls little Alex all types of motherfuckers."

"MIGUEL!"

"Get out Alex. You come over starting already." He threw his hands up in surrender and went to check on Le Le and Camila.

"I love you Miguel and be careful."

"Always and I love you too. Keep my son in your stomach until I come back." She was almost nine months and I didn't want to miss his birth.

"I'll try. I can't promise if my side nigga comes to get some, he'll stay in."

"Morgan, you want me to kill you now? You know I'll do it and go on with my life as if you never existed."

"You want to ask me a bout a threesome but I can't mention a side nigga."

"Yup. You can't beat me so I can say what I want."

"Bye Miguel." I pulled her in for a kiss.

"I'll call you when I land."

"Don't forget baby."

"He won't damn. Y'all are both stalkers of each other. I swear if either of you ever cheated, all you would do is talk about the other and make the side piece say fuck this." We both busted out laughing. He was right though.

"You ready to bring your wife home?" I asked when we stepped on the jet.

"I guess." I looked at him.

"What? Me and the kids have been bonding; plus its been quiet and I don't have to deal with her fake, boss attitude."

"You say all that but you married her and ain't letting her go."

"You damn right."

"What are you going to have her do to make up for this? I know its something with your petty ass."

"Oh she's going to be sucking a lot of dick when she gets home." I laughed so hard; my ass went into a cough attack. Alex was dead ass serious and I don't blame him.

"What you doing here?" I asked Ricky who was sitting on the jet.

"Joy asked me to go to the states and check on AJ."

"What happened to him?"

"The cops called him in for questioning yesterday about Shayla's mom disappearing and she hasn't heard from him. He told her not to come over in case they try to arrest her." I'm not sure why they were looking for her. Joy tortured the hell out of her and took her life.

"I'll make some calls when we land."

"She's scared and had me up half the night trying to figure out where he was. I'm taking a nap until we get there." Ricky did what he said and took his ass to sleep. Alex nudged him when we landed and we stepped off the plane. CJ was standing outside a truck with James Jr. I wasn't comfortable fucking with my cousin but its his death if he tries anything remotely as stupid like that again.

After he regained his movement back, CiCi had the people come over to replace his other arm with a prosthetic, so he could take care of his daughter better. He did call me and at first, I wouldn't take his calls. Morgan held out on the pussy until I did. She's known him just as long and felt he was truly sorry. I told her if he messed up again, I'm taking it out on her. Anyway, I understood why he did it, but I also told him he was too old to still feel the need of a mothers love. His ass should've never been that weak to go against family.

"Is she still there?" I asked Baako on the phone. I had him following his mother and at first he couldn't find her. He thought she disappeared when he brought Armond to me. That was until someone said they saw her hop on the plane.

"Yup." He said and I had James Jr. put the address in the GPS and head to the destination.

Gabby

I could hear his voice but because my eye was swollen shut and the other one barely opened, I couldn't see him. My body felt like a truck ran over it and smelled horrible. I tried to call out to make sure he saw me, however, my voice was no longer there due to the tremendous amount of screaming I had been doing. I laid there listening to him speak and prayed that he'd find me.

"Well, well, well. If it isn't Akeena. The bitch who was sold to a traffic ring, set free by some young nigga and the one who thought beating on my sister in law was ok."

"How... did you... find me...?" The fear in her voice was evident as MJ spoke.

"It shouldn't matter." I heard him speak to someone in Spanish and heard footsteps retreat up the steps.

"You caused a lot of havoc over here in the states and my country as well. Luckily, no one died by your hands or any hands you put in place. Do you know why that is?"

"Why?"

"Because you're not smart enough to be a BOSS." I heard him laugh.

"It doesn't matter now because I've gotten my revenge."

"Listen to how stupid you sound. The person who had you thrown in the horrible place you were, isn't even here. Yea, you may have made her daughter feel some pain but the whole thing about revenge, is to actually get the person who did you wrong. They can't feel any pain you inflicted on their daughter, which to me don't look like shit but a few beatings and a haircut."

"Fuck you MJ. Your father started this entire thing and I'm going to be the one who takes it away." I heard something click and then a bunch of people running down the steps.

"Oh you thought the bomb was going to go off?" I heard some clicks over and over. I guess she planned on killing all of us.

"Gabby. What the fuck?" I heard my husband say and then a loud thud.

"Alex really. You knocked her out before I could tell her the bomb was deactivated. Now it won't be fun." I felt my body being lifted.

"Yo, shoot those chains off her ankles." I heard the noise but kept my head buried in his chest.

"Drive this motherfucker fast to the hospital." He yelled out and the person did what he asked. I passed out after he said that.

****

"Hand me my son before I whoop your ass." I heard Alex saying as I opened my eyes.

"Take his spoiled ass. I love Lourdes ass more anyway. Ain't that right sweetie?" I thought it was Ricky's voice but there was no way in hell he'd be in my hospital room.

"Aye! Don't fucking play. You better love both of my damn kids with your punk ass." When I got my eyes all the way open, sure enough he sat there with my daughter on his lap.

"Alex." I was able to get out.

"Its about time you woke up." He kissed me on the lips.

"How long have I been asleep and why is he in here?" I heard Ricky suck his teeth.

"You been down for two days and he brought his ass here to apologize." I had to smirk.

"I don't know what you're smirking for. I'm only here because he won't let me see my God babies if I don't."

"God babies?" I questioned.

"Yup and he already asked so don't think you're going to take it back. Anyway, I apologize for snapping on you. However, I meant what I said about if you hurt him again."

"That's an apology? I'd hate to see what a real one is."

"Yo Gabby, don't start no shit. Your ass needs to apologize too." I rolled my eyes.

271

"Alex you need to divorce her petty ass. Here you done saved her and she still acting like you need to kiss her ass. What do you see in her?"

"Give me a minute everyone." I heard him say. I looked around and saw everyone else in the room. My eye had been on those two and my kids the entire time; I never realized other people were in the room. MJ, Morgan, my brother, Joy and even my mom were here.

"When you're finished I need to speak with her in private." My mom said in a way that told me she was mad. My mom grabbed my son from Alex and walked out with everyone else.

"Lets get some things straight before we go any further." He pulled the chair up next to my bed.

"First off… you will apologize to my cousin and in a respectable way. I don't ever want to hear either one of you speaking to each other the way you did at the party."

"Really. Did you hear how he?-"

"I'm sorry to say that his apology, is as good as it gets. Shit, you're lucky he even said that much."

"Second... If this is how you're going to be for the rest of your life, I'm going to need your signature right here on the dotted line."

"What's this?" I didn't touch the pen or paper.

"Annulment papers."

"Alex."

"Don't Alex me. I love you Gabby, don't get me wrong but I refused to live my life this way. There are millions of women out here who would love to take your place and truly appreciate a nigga."

"Cocky much."

"I'm not cocky but I am a good dude and the way you treat me is fucked up. If I was beating, belittling, degrading or treating you like shit, I'd expect this type of shit, but I don't. You've embarrassed me in front of my family and for what? Huh? I give you any and everything you can possibly want or need. I've never cheated on you and you're the mother of my kids." I could hear his anger rising in his voice.

"You know what? I can't do this anymore. Sign the papers."

"I'm trying Alex, I swear I am. I don't know how to stop being this way. The only relationship I had was with him and it made me build a wall. I don't know how to take down." I started crying.

"Maybe we should cool it for a while so you can get yourself together." He went to leave. I grabbed his arm and yanked him back as hard as I could with the little strength I had.

"Please don't leave me. I need you in my life Alex." He didn't say anything and stood there staring. He wiped my tears and kissed my forehead.

"Your mom wants to come in." I nodded and laid my head on the pillow as I watched my soon to be ex husband walk out the door.

"GET UP!" I didn't even bother to address her tone of voice and did what she said. She held one of my hands and Brea held the other one. She walked in with my mom with her big stomach. None of us spoke a word as I showered, brushed my teeth, cleaned my face and put on a sweat suit. I walked out the bathroom and housekeeping had just finished putting clean sheets on. I sat in the chair because I felt cooped up in the bed.

"Are you going to stay married or not?" My mom asked.

"I want to but he doesn't. I messed up ma and I don't know how to fix it. He had annulment papers drawn up already and.-" I was now crying really hard. Brea passed me some tissue and my mom sat on the bed in front of me.

"Gabriela, if you want to save your marriage, you're not only going to have to change but suck a lot of dick."

"OH MY GOD MA! YOU DID NOT JUST SAY THAT!" I had to stop her. I did not want to have a sex talk with her.

"Girl please. Why you think your father hasn't gone anywhere?"

"Spare me please aunty, I'm pregnant and I don't want to get sick."

"Was you sick when you swallowed Mateo sperm?" Brea rolled her eyes.

"Exactly! Stop acting like I'm a hundred years old. I love having sex with my husband and I'll suck the skin right off his dick."

"I'm gone. I can't right now." Brea stood up and my mom started cracking up.

"Ok Listen. Besides that and having a ton of make up sex, you're going to have to get over the shit PJ did and treat Alex better. Gabby, I raised you to be your own person and to never be weak for a man. However, you can't treat him the way someone else treated you; especially when he isn't the one who hurt you." She moved off the bed and kneeled in front of me.

"Honey that man is in love with you and I hate to say it but you're going to miss out on a good one."

"Gabby, Mateo told me he is serious about leaving you. If you can't let the wall down and love him, let him go. He deserves for a woman to treat him right." Brea said and walked out.

"Sweetie no one is trying to be mean but you have a choice to make." I climbed in the bed and laid there.

"Give it a few days and think about what we're telling you. I'm going to tell everyone to go home because you were tired." I wiped my eyes and told her thank you. I had a lot to think about and its only right to be alone as I do it.

****

Two days went by and I didn't see Alex but my parents made sure to bring my babies up everyday. I missed them so much and enjoyed every second with them. My daughter was attached to my dad already. I told him she was going to be just like me. My mom said AJ's daughter is the same. AJ's son was attached to my mom, while mine was stuck on his father.

Once they left, I took a shower and laid in the bed to watch a movie on the laptop my father brought up. He said hospital televisions only gave you the bare minimum of channels and his daughter should be able to watch what she wants. Yup, at the tender age of twenty, I'm still a daddy's girl and proud of it.

The doctors told me I could go home tomorrow and a bitch was happy as hell. The swelling had gone down in both eyes and the only issue I had, was a few bruised ribs from the kicks to my side. They wanted me to stay a few days because seizures ran in my family and they had to be sure I wouldn't have one.

I was also in a rush to get back to my husband and tell him I'm ready to be the woman he needs. I could text or call him but I'd rather do it face to face. I fell asleep watching Jeepers Creepers 2 on Netflix and woke up to someone lying next to me. I turned over and it was Alex.

"You ok?" He asked when I stood to use the bathroom.

"Yea." I closed the door to my room and went to handle my business. I brushed my teeth and made sure I looked presentable.

"ALEX!" I screamed making him come running in.

"What's wrong Gabby?" I pushed him against the wall and kissed him aggressively, as I unfastened his jeans. I was in a rush just in case he decided to stop me. I know sex and blowjobs won't fix our problems but right now, it was doing the job.

"Shit Gab. Ahhh damn it feels good." I felt his hands roaming in my hair, as he pumped slowly in and out my mouth. I spit on the tip and made it wet and sloppy.

"I'm about to cum baby. Stand up." I didn't move and soon after felt his sperm coating my throat.

"Alex, baby."

"Shhhhh." He now had my back against the wall, with my leg on his shoulders making me moan as he devoured me like a meal. I didn't care how loud I was.

"Ahhh fuck!" My body jerked a little when he entered me forcefully.

"You want me to stop."

"No. Shittttt." I came again and he laughed.

"Alex, I'm sorry for everything. I promise to be a better wife just don't leave me." He stopped and stared.

"We in this until death do us part." He stuck his tongue in my mouth and went back to beating my pussy up.

"You know you're probably pregnant again?" He said after we finished, cleaned ourselves up and laid in the bed together.

"As long as you're the father, I don't mind." He turned my face to his.

"I'm not him Gabby. Stop trying to make me pay for his mistakes."

"I know."

"Do you?"

"Yes and I know I have to apologize to quite a few people too; starting with Ricky and your mom."

"Gabby, I know my cousin comes off rough but he is a good dude. Shit, if you ever get on his good side, he'll have your back before mine. Don't ever disrespect him like that again and he knows to never do you that way either. I love both of y'all and I will go to war with him if he comes for you in any way. It doesn't mean fuck with him about his sexuality either. He is comfortable in his own skin and I'll be damned if anyone makes him feel differently."

"I get it."

"Good because his ass is our permanent babysitter when we need to go out, if his ass ain't coming."

"What about your mom?"

"You're going to give daddy a lot of head to make up for the shit you pulled at the party."

"What does that have to do with your mom?"

"A lot. I'm the one who has to convince her to like you again. In order to do that, you have to make it worth it." I busted out laughing.

"Oh yea. How about I start now?"

"Shit. You ain't said nothing but a word." He went over to the bathroom, opened the door and made it so if anyone tried to come in they couldn't because it was blocked. He came over to me and dropped his clothes.

"I'll gladly give you whatever you want but first I need to do this." I stood up and slid his ring back on. He left it on the annulment papers the day he walked out.

"I was wondering where it was." I shook my head laughing, then sat up on the bed, pulled him in closer and gave him exactly what he needed.

Morgan

I had my son a few days after we returned from the states a month and a half ago. When MJ told me how they found Gabby, I rushed over to be by her side. However, I didn't appreciate the way she treated Alex when she woke up. I understand she's gone through a lot and if Alex was a fuck nigga, I'd be all for the way she did him but he wasn't. He truly loved her and I don't think she knew how to love him back.

After she was discharged from the hospital, Alex brought her here and she apologized to everyone; on her own. I know he told her she had to eventually but I guess she wanted to get it out the way. His mom and Ricky had a hard time accepting it but did on the strength of Alex. Don't think they didn't threaten her over it. I hoped she learned her lesson because I honestly don't see him taking her back if she does it again.

****

Two days from today, I would be remarrying my husband. I couldn't wait to walk down the aisle in my dress that was made in Paris. It was pretty expensive but Miguel said not to worry about the price on anything. His mom even had the people at Jimmy Choo, design my shoes since those are my favorite. Joy brought me a pair of diamond earrings to wear with the dress and they were beautiful.

"Shit Morgan. Fuck, I needed that." MJ said after I gave him head before going out with the girls for my bachelorette party.

"Why you think I gave it to you? I always know what you need."

"I know what you need to." He lifted me up and tossed me on the bed. My legs were damn near touching my ears, as he pounded in and out of me.

"Miguel, I love this dick. Yes baby, right there. Oh my Godddddddd." I yelled out and came again. It didn't stop him from putting a hurting on me for the next hour or however long it was.

"Have fun baby." He kissed me on the way out the door. His bachelor party was last night. He brought his ass home pissy drunk and couldn't even make it up the stairs.

"I will."

"You know he showing up right?" Ricky said after I closed the door.

"Yup. Its ok though. I plan on being on my best behavior." Ricky looked at me.

"After he gets there though. Before he comes, is another story."

"I know that's right. Lets go see some dang a lang, swang." I loved hanging out with Ricky. He was carefree and a breath of fresh air.

"Do we have to pick her up?" He asked pulling into Alex's driveway.

"Yes and you accepted the apology so move on. Its my night and I don't want no shit Ricky." He sucked his teeth as Gabby came towards the car.

"Ricky, if you fuck with my wife, I'm fucking you up. The same goes for you Gabby but in a different way." He kissed her on the lips and closed the door.

"What the fuck ever. I'll just make sure not to tell you if she's swinging on a strippers dick." Alex ran to the other side of the car but Ricky pulled off.

We pulled up to the club a little after ten and met Joy, Zariah who had her baby three weeks ago, Savannah, my mom, Miguel's mom, his aunt Hazel, his grandmothers and everyone else we knew. My best friend Patience even came over to celebrate along with her mom. Once I walked in, I noticed all of Miguel's jersey family too, including the guys.

"Why are the guys here?" I asked and Violet led me to an area that was decorated with Bride To Be on it. There was champagne, gift bags for everyone who came, a few bags were from Prada, Gucci, and from a few other expensive stores on the table too.

"Honey, tonight is all about you." My mom said and handed me a bag. I opened it and there were a few sex toys and a see through Teddy in it.

"I need a drink before I open any more gifts." I picked up one of the shots off the waitress tray and took it to the head.

The next bag and those after that I opened had more lingerie in it, sex toys, handcuffs, blindfolds, triple X videos and so much other sexual shit, I had no idea existed. I'm sure all of it won't be used but most of it will. Me and my man were freaks in the bedroom, that's for sure.

We sat there drinking for the next hour when the DJ announced it was time for the strippers to come out. I looked around to make sure Miguel wasn't there, so I could act up for a minute. I made it downstairs with everyone behind me. The guys were no longer there and women swarmed the floor. The song Pony, by Ginuwine came on and the first stripper came out. That is one song that never gets old.

He made his way around the circle. This man was built in all the right places and knew how to move his body. He came over to me and began dancing. His dick was in my face as he went along with the music. My hands were on his chest until I saw him being yanked away. My husband is a fucking mess.

"He can dance over there." Miguel said and walked off. I knew he'd be there but damn, I thought I'd get to act up a little. The stripper looked petrified and so did the one who came out after him.

"You make me sick." I said to him as he sat at the bar. I decided to leave the dance floor because the strippers were scared and I wanted all the women to enjoy themselves.

"He shouldn't have been that close." He shrugged his shoulders. I sat on the stool with my back leaning against the bar watching the women. Both of our moms were having a good time. I almost lost it when I saw his abuela letting the stripper hump on her.

"That's what your ass gets. You did the same shit at my bachelorette party. The only difference is, you beat the stripper up. You should be happy I didn't do that." I laughed because I did show up at his party.

At first no one knew we were there due to all the men lusting over the half naked women. It seemed to be going alright and I was getting ready to leave until some of the guys started yelling. Me, Ricky and Joy went to see what it was about and I'll be damned if some chick didn't have her leg on my husbands shoulder as she pretended to fuck his face.

I snatched that bitch back and beat her ass. Before I left, I made it known to the rest of those hoes he was off limits and better not even think about walking in front of him with their ass hanging out. For the rest of the night, all Miguel did was drink and I know that because Ryan told it to Ricky. That's why his ass was so damn drunk.

"Baby, her pussy was in your face."

"And his dick was in yours."

"Fine. If its going to be like that, the least you can do is give me some dick in the bathroom."

"Oh you ain't said nothing. Lets go." He grabbed me off the seat and tossed me over his shoulder.

"Look at this shit." he pointed to my mom and his aunt Hazel double-teaming one of the strippers.

"They're having fun."

"Whatever. Strip." He closed the bathroom door and I gave him a strip show off the music playing. By the time my clothes came off he was hard as a rock and had a big grin on his face.

"I'm going to have to pay you for your services."

"Yes you will and no bills less than a hundred. This pussy right here is worth millions or should I say billions now that we're married."

"Try trillions baby and you're wrong. No money in the world is enough to pay for what's in between your legs. Now let me fuck my stripper wife."

"You better."

****

I woke up the next day hung over with a sore ass pussy. Mind you, we had sex before my party and again in the bathroom, where he fucked me so good, I had to be carried out. I was so embarrassed because everyone kept asking if I were ok and Miguel's ignorant ass told them why. Of course, Ricky talked shit and Patience couldn't stop laughing.

"Baby, I have to go. I'll see you later." Miguel said kissing my lips and running out the door.

"Bitchhhhhh, get your lazy ass up." Ricky said barging in my room with Gabby, Patience and Joy behind him.

"Why are y'all up so early?" I got up and went to relieve my bladder.

"Girl, its after three." Patience said coming in and starting the shower.

"Damn, its that late?"

"Yea. Get your ass ready because you're getting married tomorrow and our nail appointments are today." I told her ok, did what I had to do and we were gone.

"Have you seen my daughter?" Some woman asked as we stepped in the nail salon. She handed each of us a photo and it was Julia, who was Alex's ex. Gabby sucked her teeth and tossed the paper in the trash, which was a dumb thing to do.

"Excuse me. Did you know Julia? I noticed you sucked your teeth and tossed the flyer out."

"She's not from here." Ricky said and pulled her away. Julia's mom gave us a crazy look but walked away.

"You may not have cared for Julia but keep those feelings inside. You have the man as your husband." Joy told her and Ricky chimed in.

"Exactly! You'll see a lot of missing people flyers and even if you do or don't know them, give the person some respect. Regardless of how they died, that's still their family member." We had been trying to school Gabby on how to handle herself. We weren't trying to run her life but you can't go around snapping on people for no reason either.

The rest of the day went fine as we finished at the salon, went out to eat and shop. When we got home it was after nine and a bitch was tired. I checked in on my girls and my son who had been home with abuela all day and then went to take a shower.

I opened the bedroom door and almost cried at what I saw. There were pink roses in a few vases around the room, a huge teddy bear that had the words I love you on the stomach, more gift bags from Versace and Christian Louboutin. I picked the envelope up and there were two tickets to the Cayman Islands and a small note.

I hope you like everything in this room and before you say its too much, its not. Morgan you are worth this and so much more. I am going to give you the world, well what I haven't already and spoil you until I take my last breath. You are my one and only true love. I love you baby and I can't wait to meet you at the altar tomorrow. I sat on the bed crying for a few minutes and picked my phone up.

Me: *I love you more baby and I can't wait to meet you at the altar tomorrow too.*

My husband: *Goodnight baby.*

I put my phone down and got myself ready for bed. Even though we were married, it still felt like tomorrow would be my first wedding.

MJ

"Make sure all of that is in the house." I told the security dude at the gate. I handed him the stuff I brought for Morgan. I wanted to be there when she got home but one... I had to handle something and two... she's told me on plenty of occasions not to see her the day before.

"I'm on my way now to do it." I pulled off and drove to the spot where he was being held.

On the way over, I thought about how everything in my life was perfect. I had my kids, my wife, my life and my family. We've gone through a lot in the last few years but it made all of us stronger. Mostly all of us had kids now and for those who didn't, they had some on the way.

James Jr. had a daughter on the way by his girlfriend of five years and Darius had one on the way too by some chick none of us met. CJ met some woman who was a nurse as well and they seemed to be doing great. He did have me do an extensive check on her to make sure she wasn't related and working with any enemies.

Zariah welcomed her daughter with Akeem who was ecstatic and I swear sent us photos of her and Jacob damn near everyday. DJ had his twins by Savannah and asked her to marry him and she accepted. Patience was pregnant again and her boyfriend Alex Jr. finally got up the nerve to ask Cream for her hand in marriage. He gave him a hard time but gave in. Ricky and Ryan adopted a newborn daughter, which was a bad idea because all Ricky did was dress her up and told everyone she was the new diva in the family.

Overall, we had a tight knit family and no one expected any of Miguel and Violet's kids to live this long. I say that because some thought with me taking the throne, I'd fail or be assassinated. My father taught me well, so for those who are disappointed to see me excel, I say fuck em.

I pulled in the parking lot and saw Alex's car along with the few ones from the house, which meant everyone came. I opened the door and found some of them drinking and others watching television. I asked where my brother was since he was missing and they pointed to the room I didn't think he'd be in yet.

"You good." I asked as he had the chainsaw cutting off PJ's legs. He came home as I was leaving from killing Akeena. Imagine his surprise when he saw me in his house. Oh he begged and pleaded for his life, which was funny to me since he claimed to be tough. The crazy part is, he didn't even do that much begging for his kids. Alex had been torturing him the entire time and today was the day he would finally get rid of him.

"Yup. Go in the other room and enjoy yourself. You're wedding is tomorrow." I closed the door and joined the card game that was now in session. Alex came out the room an hour later asking for a beer. We all ended up leaving around three in the morning. I walked in my parents' house and my pops was still up.

"I'm proud of you son. You, Alex, Joy, Mariana, Andres are all doing very well."

"Thanks."

"Don't cheat on her son." He said as I went to walk away.

"I won't pops. I almost lost her for good once and I can't go through that shit again." He nodded his head and headed upstairs with me. We said goodnight and went into separate bedrooms. I sent my wife another text and took my ass to sleep.

****

I woke up after feeling someone jumping on the bed. It was my sister Allanah telling me my mom told her to wake me up. I grabbed her and started tickling her. She screamed for me to stop. I pushed her off the bed and ran in the bathroom; locking the door behind me. My sister pounded and kicked the door a few times trying to get me. She is going to be just like Joy when she grows up. Evil and dangerous.

The day seemed to fly by and it was now time for my wedding. I stood at the altar with my best man, who was my brother Alex, and all my groomsman, which were all my cousins. The music started and the bridesmaids, flower girls and our parents came down the aisle. When I laid eyes on Morgan, I had to take a deep breath. She has always been beautiful but today I couldn't even explain what she looked like. There were really no words to explain her.

Her dress was strapless, fitted and had diamond looking things on it. The train was long and some chick was fixing it as she stepped in the church. I couldn't see her face clearly but I could tell she was already crying, which made me catch my own from falling. She stopped in front of me; I lifted her veil and waited for the reverend to start the ceremony. When he asked us did we want to do our own vows, we both said yes, and I let her go first.

"Miguel, you and I have known each other for quite some time. You were my first crush, gave me my first kiss and you are my first love. In the years that we lost touch, I tried to get over you and find someone else but it wasn't in my cards. No man came close to having my heart the way you do." I wiped the few tears coming down her face and listened to her finish.

"I didn't know loving you could be like this. I find myself wanting to be with you every second of the day. I know in my heart, there's a place in me that belongs to you. My heart is content with you as my best friend, my lover and my husband. There's no other man who will ever come before you. I promise to love you unconditionally and not run away at the first sign of trouble. I've waited so long for this moment and I'm overjoyed that you chose me to bare your children and be your wife. I love you baby."

"Ma. Pass me some tissue." I handed it to Morgan and lifted her face to stare at me. Shit, if she crying now, she's going to be balling when I'm finished.

"You ok for me to say mine?" She nodded her head. I asked my mom for more tissue.

"Morgan, you are my best friend, my lover and wife. Before you came back into my life, I was reckless with women and didn't care about their feelings. You ruined my philosophy on them and made me see things differently. When I lost you, it felt as if you took my heart with you and it wasn't beating the way it should have been. People think men don't have feelings but they do and I'm not ashamed to admit that I shed tears for you."

"Miguel." She whispered my name and I asked her to let me finish.

"I never thought I could settle down but you changed all of that. I knew you were the one for me and it's the reason God placed you in my life for the second time. I promise to never cheat or abuse you. I'll never find anyone more precious than you and I don't want to. You are my everything and I want to spend the rest of my life being the man you crave, the man you can't sleep without, the man who makes you laugh, and the only one who makes you scream." I heard a few laughs.

"Thank you for sticking it out with me. I love you Morgan and I'm happy you said yes." Morgan had so many tears coming down her face, she couldn't see.

"Da da." I looked down and Camila was standing by my leg and Le Le was behind her. Alex picked both of them up and handed Le Le to DJ, who was next to him. The reverend waited for Morgan to gain her composure and finished the ceremony.

"By the power invested in me, I pronounce you husband and wife. Again." I pulled her closer and kissed her in a sensual, yet erotic way.

"I'm getting you pregnant again on our honeymoon." I whispered in her ear before we walked down the aisle. She smiled.

After the reception, we hopped on the jet to go on our honeymoon and were in the bed before he even pulled off. You would think it was the first time we had sex by the way we tore one another's clothes off.

"I love you Morgan Rodriquez."

"I love you too Miguel Rodriquez. I think we should stay in for the entire honeymoon to make sure I get pregnant again."

"Are you serious?"

"Yup. But you have some potent sperm, and I can bet they're already fighting for a spot." I had to laugh.

"You damn right. Lets hope for some twins."

"Oh no Miguel. We already have a set, and five kids is a bit much."

"Nothing is too much for us. You are the perfect woman and if we had ten kids, I know you'll still be the best mother to them."

"Nice try Miguel. You won't talk me into making a bet about having that many kids."

"Whatever. Don't act like you know me." She pulled my face to hers.

"I know you very well baby and don't you forget it."

The End....

Coming Soon!!

Creepin' With

The Plug

Sneek Peek

Prologue…

Camari

"Please don't do this Camari. We go way back." Sean cried out as Jermaine and Mark held him upside down from the top of the abandoned building.

"Tsk, Tsk, Tsk. Sean where was this way back shit you talking when the FEDS snatched you up and hid you in witness protection to snitch on me and my operation?"

"I'm sorry man. Come on, I have a family and.-"

"Bring him up." I told them and stepped back as they stood him on the ground. He had to hold on to the wall because he was dizzy from the blood rushing to his brain in that position. I moved closer to him and sniffed. I looked down and the nigga had shit running down his pants, with a piss stain in the front.

"Where was the concern about your family when they had you in hiding? You didn't reach out to them and had a nigga taking care of them. Granted, I believed something happened to you as well until my lawyer showed me a discovery with your name on it." He put his head down.

"Imagine my surprise when I found out a nigga who was eating lovely, worked with the pigs." He remained silent and that only pissed me off more. I hit him so hard in the mouth you could hear his jaw crack.

"I have to say Sean, you had me fooled but the joke was on you because once I found out, me and my boys here, took turns with your wife. Unfortunately, she wasn't good at sucking dick nor was she a good lay. Mannnn, how did you stay with her so long?" We all started laughing. You could see the anger in his face as he held his mouth with blood dripping out.

"Look, I'm going to give you a chance to redeem yourself and possibly save your family because you're not walking out of here alive." His eyes grew wide.

"Come on Sean. Don't give me that look. You know the consequences of disloyalty." He nodded his head.

"I want you to nod yes or no when I ask this question. I already know the truth so your answer will decided the fate of your wife and kids." I watched Jermaine remove his weapon from his waist.

One thing I didn't do was murder. I've had my share of bodies but now that I'm a boss and run the Midwest, I never got my hands dirty. Oh, don't get it twisted. I'm the one who put the hits out. I also made sure I was in attendance each time, to make sure the person was dead because I trusted no one when it came to that. People start feeling bad and let the person live, which allows them to run or even snitch. I have too much shit going on to let someone from my camp slip up.

I watched Jermaine walk up to Sean, place the gun on his head and tell him to get on his knees. I could've tossed him over the edge but I needed to see his face when he took his last breathe. Call it crazy, but in certain situations there are some things you wanted to see yourself. Sean did what he asked and looked up at me with pleading eyes.

"Did you give the FEDS all the information about my operation?" I knew the answer and wanted to see if he spoke truthfully. Sean wasn't a corner boy and knew a lot about how I ran my business. He knew about drop-offs, shipments, pickups, some murders, my gambling ring and a bunch off other things. That's why I changed shit up when he went missing. I may have assumed something bad happened to him but until I was sure, changes were made. I'm glad I went with my gut because it all came out.

"Thank you for the truth." I said once he nodded his head yes. Jermaine went to pull the trigger but I stopped him.

"Don't worry about your family Sean. They were already dead before you were brought here. Night, night nigga." I said and watched his body drop after he was hit with two to his dome.

"Make sure this shit is cleaned up and meet me at the place. You already know what we're about to do." I told them smiling.

I made the call to this chick Nancy I had been fucking as of lately and told her to get two of her friends and meet me at the hotel. Whenever we *had* to handle something of this nature, we always needed something to unwind us, and what better way than with sex. I got in the car and gave my driver my destination. I put my head back on the seat and thought about how this case too, would go away.

"What you thinking bro?" Jermaine asked when we got to the hotel. I was standing outside the car waiting on him and Mark, who drove his own car as well.

"I'm not sure about the shit with Sean. Something is funny with him."

"What you mean?"

"I'm saying. Sean definitely had a high position but the information I read on the discovery is high class shit that only a few of us know." We both turned around and looked at Mark who took forever to get out his car.

"Camari look. We've been boys since elementary school so when I see shit, I say something. Right before we got to the top of the roof.-"

"Y'all ready." Jermaine stopped talking. Whatever he had to tell me, either he didn't want Mark to know, or Mark was involved somehow.

"Yea we good." I said and gave Jermaine the side eye.

"I'm about to tear some pussy up." Mark rubbed his hands together like a kid about to get candy.

"Y'all go ahead. Tell Nancy I apologize for inconveniencing her and I'll hit her up tomorrow."

"You good." Mark asked as he walked backwards to the door.

"I have some things I need to handle. Have a good time." Without another word, he left Jermaine and I standing there. I was about to ask what he was talking about earlier but decided against it. When the time is right, Jermaine will tell me.

"We'll talk tomorrow." I gave Jermaine a pound and got in the car.

"Take me to Carol Street." My driver pulled off and headed in the direction of my house in the hills that no one knew of, not even my boys.

The entire drive over all I could think about was how Mark would die if I found out he was the one who's been giving out information. I don't give a fuck how long we've been friends; the one thing I don't fuck with, is a disloyal nigga. I think its time for me to get my hands dirty again and I know just who I'm going to start with first.

Coming Soon!!

CPSIA information can be obtained
at www.ICGtesting.com
Printed in the USA
LVOW13s1050250218
567697LV00017B/602/P